KILL FACTOR

BRIAN BOWYER

Copyright © 2024 Brian Bowyer

Cover art by Don Noble of Rooster Republic Press
First edition 2023 publication by Potter Grove Press
Additional designs by editor Paige Johnson of Outcast Press

www.Outcast-Press.com

(print): ISBN: 978-1-960882-09-7

ALSO BY BRIAN BOWYER

OLD TOO SOON

SCARLETT

GRINDING ROAD

FLESH REHEARSAL

AUTUMN GOTHIC

ALIVE UNDEAD

SINISTER MIX

APOCALYPSE

ROAD HARVEST

SHELF LIFE

WRITING AND RISING

FROM ADDICTION

CH. I

In the psych ward's day room, Lemarcus played solitaire while the other freaks watched TV. Detecting motion from the corner of his eye, he turned his head to the left and saw the white dude—who hadn't spoken since his arrival two weeks ago—rise from a chair and slash an orderly's throat with a piece of glass.

Broken coffee pot, probably, Lemarcus thought.

The orderly—Lemarcus could not remember his name—was a mean son of a bitch, and he didn't go down easily. He stood 6'6 and weighed about two-sixty of mostly muscle. Arterial blood shot across the ward's white floor as one of the female patients screamed and ran from the path of the orderly's gushing carotid.

Lemarcus didn't mind watching the orderly flounder.

He was a brutish, disrespectful bastard who enjoyed humiliating and intimidating the patients. Now, he scrambled on his feet with both hands clamped across his throat, trying to stop the pouring blood. He shot Lemarcus a look, his eyes begging for mercy, and Lemarcus gave him both middle fingers.

"Go to Hell, punk," Lemarcus told him.

The rest of the patients in the day room either continued watching TV or observed the orderly dying with indifference.

"Please," he croaked. "Somebody. Please—"

Then he dropped to the floor, bled out, and died.

The white dude unclipped the key ring from the orderly's belt, took a set of car keys from his pocket, and snatched his wallet.

Apparently, the white dude had been paying attention the past two weeks, for he knew which key got him out of the ward. He moved like a predator, swiftly but discreet, and Lemarcus could tell he stayed in shape just by looking at him.

Silently, Lemarcus followed behind him in his hospital slippers.

When he got to a security station, where a guard sat filling out paperwork and flirting with a nurse who stood in front of his desk, the white dude rushed up behind the nurse and pressed his shiv to her neck.

"Put your gun on the desk," the white dude told the security guard, "or I'll cut her fucking throat."

The security guard—a slender, middle-aged black man—apparently believed the white dude's words. "No problem, fella. I'm reaching for my gun right now. Just take it easy. Don't hurt her. I'm gonna set the gun on my desk."

After the guard set his pistol—a Glock 9mm—on the desk, the white dude picked it up, put the muzzle to the nurse's head, and headed toward an exit.

Lemarcus followed.

When the white dude reached the door, he unlocked it, tossed aside the shiv, and told the nurse to get lost.

She took off running down the hall.

Then the white dude turned to Lemarcus, gun raised. "Why are you following me?"

"Because I need to get the fuck out of here. My wife had me committed, but she's the goddamn psycho, and now she has my daughter. You can use me as a hostage if you want to. It might help."

The white dude shrugged. "Maybe so." Then he gestured toward the door. "After you."

The white dude followed him out the door, which opened up onto the back lawn, a groundskeeper's shed, and the staff parking lot.

While crossing the lawn, the white dude pressed a button on the orderly's key fob. Instantly, an SUV tweeted, and its hazard lights flashed twice.

They rushed to it and the white dude told Lemarcus, "You're driving."

"No problem."

They got in.

Lemarcus started the engine and put it in drive, feeling weird to be sitting behind a steering wheel in pajamas, a robe, and hospital slippers.

"We'll have to crash through the gate and outrun security," the white dude said. "I'm Austin, by the way. What's your name?"

"Lemarcus."

"It's nice to meet you, Lemarcus. Are you familiar with this area?"

"Yep. Born and raised right here in Warlington. Went to school at Alcorn State in Mississippi, but moved back here to West Virginia after I graduated."

"So, you can outrun security? You can lose them if they come after us?"

"We damn sure about to find out."

Lemarcus circled the lot once, then floored it, headed for the gate. No employees or visitors were coming in or out, so the gate was shut. At the last second, he glanced over at two guards in the security booth—both of whom appeared to realize what was happening. Then he smashed into the gate and drove through.

Austin turned around to look behind them. "They're not chasing us."

"Nope. They're undoubtedly calling the cops right now."

"There's a state police station about two miles up the road," Austin said, "on Eisenhower Drive. They'll be setting up roadblocks in no time."

"I know. We gotta swap this car for another one, pronto."

On Stanaford Road, Lemarcus floored it in the other direction, headed toward downtown.

CH. 2

Brenda knew that Allen was in love with her. She was certain of it. Whenever he told her, "Brenda, stop calling me," what he really meant was, "Brenda, don't stop calling me." It was maddening, really, how he couldn't say what he really meant with his bitch-ass wife Pamela looking over his shoulder.

When Brenda had worked in Allen's office, life was beautiful. She would bake him cakes, buy him candy, and give him ice cream, and he would smile at her in a way that meant, *I love you, Brenda, even though I'm married and therefore unable to tell you how much I love you. You're so beautiful, and I want to fuck your brains out.*

It was amazing how much he could say with a single smile. Everything about him was amazing, and she wanted to spend the rest of her life with Allen.

But Pamela kept him on a leash like a goddamn puppy dog.

As Brenda stepped out of the jewelry store—with the wristwatch she had stolen for Allen as a gift inside her purse—she thought perhaps this was a mistake. She had never stolen anything this expensive before, and she half expected someone to follow her out of the store and tell her she'd been caught as she headed toward her car.

When she reached her car, she unlocked it, hands fumbling. Then she heard a man's voice behind her—but didn't understand what he said. Turning around, expecting to see a store cop or a security guard, she instead saw two men: a black guy and a white guy, each wearing pajamas and a robe.

Homeless people, Brenda thought, relieved. "Look," she told them. "I don't have any money. You're barking up the wrong tree."

"We don't want your money," the black man said. "We just need your car."

"My car?" Brenda thought the men were at least a decade younger than she was. Mid-twenties, probably. Certainly, no older than 30. "You can't have my car."

The white man pulled a gun from behind his back and aimed it at her midsection. "Get in the fucking car, bitch."

Brenda did.

CH. 3

There was something weird about the woman, but Lemarcus couldn't put his finger on it. He rode next to her on the passenger's side while she drove. Austin rode behind them, undoubtedly with the handgun pointed at her back.

"What's your name, sweetie?" Lemarcus asked her.

"Brenda. And I don't have any money in my bank account, so there's no use telling me to drive to an ATM. I lost my job recently, and I'm flat broke."

"I already told you, we don't want your money," Lemarcus said. "And I'm sorry to hear you lost your job. I lost my job recently, too, and it's no picnic. I know what you're going through."

"So, what do you want from me? Are you going to rape me?"

"Hell no, we're not gonna rape you. We just need a place to lay low for a little bit, until we figure out what to do." He pointed to Warlington General straight ahead. "So just park up there at the hospital and kill the engine."

Brenda did, blending in with a slew of other vehicles. "How did you lose your job?" she asked Lemarcus.

"Long story. I'm an alcoholic, for one thing, but that had nothing to do with it. My wife had me arrested. Said I beat her up, even though I never touched her. Then she had me committed. Said that I was a threat to her and our daughter."

"My boss's wife made him fire me," Brenda said. "His name is Allen. I'm in love with Allen, and he's in love with me. We don't see each other much now, though. Well, I do still see him outside his house sometimes. I got him a watch. Would you like to see it?" Without waiting for a response, she pulled the wristwatch from her purse and held it up.

"Nice watch," Lemarcus said. "Is that why you're broke? You spent all your money on that watch?"

"Oh, no. I couldn't afford this watch, so I stole it. I spent my last few dollars on the bottle of vodka in the trunk."

Lemarcus shot her a look. "You got a bottle of vodka in the trunk?"

"Yep. I'm an alcoholic, too. Been drinking for years."

Lemarcus smiled. "Damn, girl. You should have said something. Pop the trunk, and I'll grab us that bottle."

Brenda popped the trunk.

Lemarcus got out, grabbed the bottle, and got back in. He cracked its seal. Before he brought it to his lips, he asked Brenda, "You don't mind drinking after a black man, do you?"

She laughed, and Lemarcus thought she sounded like a maniac. "Lord, no," Brenda said. "I've been with a lot of black men, believe me. Allen's white, but my boyfriend before him was a black man."

Lemarcus took a drink, and then he took another. "Damn, that shit hits the spot after three weeks of abstinence."

Brenda put the watch back in her purse. "You haven't had a drink in three weeks?"

"Nope." He handed her the bottle. "I've been locked up in a psych ward. We both have. We just escaped. That's why we're dressed like this."

Brenda took a drink, and then turned to face Austin, who immediately raised the gun to her face. The sight of the Glock's muzzle 12 inches from her eyes didn't seem to faze her. "What about you, white boy?" she asked him, as if she weren't Caucasian. "Are you an alcoholic, too?"

Austin lowered the gun, but kept it aimed at her back. "Nope. I'm a drug addict. But I do like to drink."

She proffered the bottle. "Wanna hit this vodka?"

Austin shook his head. "Not right now. Maybe later."

"Suit yourself." She turned around, took a drink, and handed Lemarcus the bottle. "I need to get this watch to Allen," Brenda said.

Lemarcus turned around and told Austin, "We need to get some street clothes."

"I know." Pointing the gun at Brenda with one hand, Austin gave him the dead orderly's wallet with his other. "See how much is in there."

Lemarcus counted the money. "Not much. Certainly not enough to buy some clothes."

"Allen has clothes that would fit you," Brenda said. "Allen's tall and thin, just like you two."

Lemarcus shot her a look. "What? You got a key to his house, or some shit?"

"No, but he might be home. It's a Saturday afternoon, so I know he's not in his office today."

Lemarcus tossed the wallet onto the floorboard. "What are we supposed to do? Just go to his house and ring the doorbell?"

"Sure! Why not?"

Lemarcus took a drink. "What the fuck you gonna do? Hand him the watch, then tell him that we just broke out of a psych ward, carjacked your dumb ass, and need to borrow some street clothes? Get the fuck outta here."

"I actually like her plan," Austin said. "She can tell him we carjacked her as soon as she left the jewelry store, that we forced her to tell us where we can get some clothes, and that his house was the only place she could think of."

"Exactly!" Brenda said. "And if you end up killing his wife, I won't be disappointed. Her name's Pamela. I hate that fucking bitch."

Lemarcus shrugged. "Fuck it. Let's do this shit."

Fifteen minutes later, Brenda parked her car in front of the last house on Oakwood Lane. The house, a wedding-cake Victorian with two turrets and steep roofs, was decorated with millwork and flanked by white oaks.

"Nice place," Lemarcus said.

They all got out and approached the entrance. Brenda pressed the doorbell while Austin held the gun to her back.

A woman with smudged makeup opened the door, still in a nightgown. "Brenda? What the fuck are you doing here?" Then she looked at Austin and Lemarcus in their pajamas. "And who the hell are these two freaks?"

"Hello, Pamela," Brenda said. "I was carjacked, and now they need some of Allen's clothes."

"His clothes? What are you talking about?"

Austin raised the gun and pointed it at Pamela. "This is a home invasion, bitch." He shoved Brenda into the foyer, then Lemarcus followed, locking the door behind them.

Aiming the gun at her face, Austin asked Pamela, "Where's your husband?"

"He's in the living room. We were watching TV."

Austin nodded. "Lead the way. And don't do anything stupid, or I'll blow your brains out."

Pamela led them into the living room, where Lemarcus saw two white chicks fucking each other with dildos on the big-screen TV. Her husband sat on the sofa, his erection poking through the slit of his boxer shorts.

"Allen!" Brenda screamed, and then pointed at his wife. "Were you fucking this goddamn bitch?"

"Brenda?" Allen said, covering his genitals with a pillow. "What the hell are you doing here?"

What happened next, happened fast.

Lemarcus noticed the apples, grapes, and strawberries on the coffee table, but had not given them more than a cursory glance. Apparently, Pamela and her husband had been snacking on fruit while watching porn. Amidst the fruit was a tub of cream cheese, a jar of marshmallow fluff, and a paring knife to slice the apples.

Dropping her purse onto the floor, Brenda grabbed the knife and slammed it into the side of Pamela's neck. "Die, you fucking whore!" she screamed, drawing the blade across the front of her throat. When she yanked it out, arterial blood shot across the room.

"No!" Allen yelled, rising from the sofa as his wife hit the floor. He kneeled and tried to stop the bleeding, but there was nothing he could do.

She died in his arms.

Weeping, he looked up at Brenda, covered in blood. "Crazy bitch," he whispered, and then shouted, "You killed my fucking wife!"

"YOU TOLD ME YOU LOVED ME! YOU PROMISED TO LEAVE HER! I GOT YOU A WATCH AND EVERYTHING!"

Allen shook his head. "You're insane. There was never anything between us. Every bit of this was all in your mind."

"Very well." Pointing at Allen, Brenda told Austin, "Kill this piece of shit."

"How about I kill you both?" Austin said. Then he shot them once each, through the head.

"Damn, white boy!" Lemarcus said, laughing. "You're like Annie Oakley with a pistol, ain't ya?"

Austin shrugged. "Lots of practice. Let's go find some clothes."

They searched the first floor but didn't find the master bedroom.

On their way upstairs, Austin said, "I'm 6'3. How tall are you? About 6'5?"

"6'4," Lemarcus said. "And dude was about our height, so his clothes should definitely fit. What size shoes you wear?"

"12. You?"

"13."

In the master bedroom at the end of an upstairs hallway, they found more business attire than anything else in the dead man's closet. Each put on black slacks, white dress shirts, black ties, and black sports coats.

"We look like a couple of feds," Lemarcus said.

"Or gangsters," Austin countered, slipping into a pair of Oxford shoes.

Lemarcus chose a pair of gray Nike tennis shoes, size twelve. "Close enough."

Austin began riffling through some dresser drawers. "I wish we could find some cash around this place. I need to get some drugs in my system, immediately."

Lemarcus helped him search the room. "You said you're a drug addict. Which drug are you addicted to?"

Austin shot him a look. "All of them, I guess. Heroin, crack, crystal meth. Just whatever. Anything that dulls the edges of reality."

"Yeah, man. I know what you mean. Reality has some sharp fucking edges. That's why I drink." Lemarcus found some cash in a shoebox beneath the bed, and counted it. "There's $10,000 here, man. You wanna split it?"

"Sure. That will hold me over for a couple of days. Well, until my father tells me it's safe to come home, anyway."

Lemarcus shot him a look. "Damn, white boy. How old are you?"

"27."

"27? And you still live with your parents?"

"It's a big house," Austin said. "The whole family lives there. I'll tell you about it later. And trust me, I have enough cash in a safe-deposit box to buy ten houses, but it takes two keys to open—my key, and the bank's key. And I don't even have my key on me. Plus, I don't think it's a good idea to go in the bank right now, anyway... Why? How old are you?"

"28. One year older than you."

In the single drawer of the nightstand nearest the door, Lemarcus found a Glock 19 and held it up. "Check it out! It's the same kind of gun you took from the security guard."

Austin nodded. "It's a popular model. Any extra shells in that drawer?"

"Two boxes." Lemarcus shoved the pistol into the waistband around the small of his back. Then he withdrew both boxes of ammunition and handed one to Austin.

They went downstairs.

From Brenda's corpse on the floor, Austin retrieved her car keys. "Do you still feel like driving?"

"Hell yeah, white boy. I always feel like driving. Where we going?"

Austin tossed him the keys. "To get some drugs, man. I don't feel so good. I know a dealer who doesn't live too far from here. I'll show you the way."

"Cool," Lemarcus said.

They left.

CH. 4

She approached him at a rest area on I-95 in Georgia as he headed toward his car. He had been visiting his parents in Florida and was now traveling back to New York. He could tell she was beautiful despite the dark sunglasses she wore. Long, blonde hair cascaded from beneath the baseball cap on her head. She wore a blue tank top and light-blue denim shorts. A duffel bag was slung across one shoulder, and she held a suitcase in the opposite hand.

"How far north ya headed?" she asked him.

Her accent was strange; he couldn't place it.

"New York."

"Can I catch a ride with you?"

He smiled. "Absolutely. What's your name?"

"Britney."

"It's nice to meet you, Britney. I'm Zack."

He led her to his car and opened the rear passenger door. She set her suitcase in there, then got in the passenger's side up front with her duffel bag.

Zack put the car back on the road, and they headed north. "Are you going to New York, too?" he asked her.

She turned in her seat to face him, with her back against the passenger door. She pulled a pistol from her duffel bag and aimed it at him—casually, not aggressively. "I don't know yet. I haven't decided."

Zack put his eyes to the road. "Are you gonna rob me? Is that your plan?"

"No. I don't need your money. I probably have more money than you'll ever see in your life."

"Is that right?"

"Probably."

"Then why are you pointing that gun at me?"

"Maybe it's for my own protection. I mean, for all I know, you could be a rapist or a serial killer."

"That's true," Zack said. "But if you have so much money, why were you asking strangers for transportation at a rest area? Why aren't you cruising around in a Ferrari or a limousine?"

She laughed. "I actually have a Ferrari. And a limousine. But maybe I'm a serial killer. Maybe I've been traveling around America for 26 days, killing good Samaritans like yourself."

"Is that what you are? A serial killer?"

She put her gun away. "No. Of course not. But I could be." From her duffel bag, she retrieved a bottle of vodka and took a drink.

"How old are you, Britney?"

"24. You?"

"Twice your age. I'm 48."

"Oh, wow. My father's 48. Is that some old Metallica you're listening to? I can barely hear it."

"Yep." He turned up the stereo. "Their *Ride the Lightning* album, from 1984."

"It's great," Britney said. "One of my favorites."

They crossed the border into South Carolina an hour later, and Zack stopped at a gas station soon thereafter.

He killed the engine. "You going in?"

"No, but thanks for the ride." She got out and grabbed her suitcase from the back.

Zack got out, too. "Where are you going?"

"I don't know yet. Guess I'll find out when I get there."

"You're a strange one, Britney. I'll give you that. But it was nice meeting you."

"Likewise. Have a nice life."

He laughed. "I'll try."

She turned, and he watched her walk away.

CH. 5

Lemarcus drove with the bottle between his legs. Austin guided him to a small house on Larew Avenue and told him to wait in the car. While he waited, Lemarcus fantasized about killing his wife and kidnapping his daughter. He would probably get caught, of course, and spend the rest of his life in prison, but he figured his daughter would be better off in an orphanage than with her psychotic, pill-addicted mother.

Austin got back in, holding a brown paper bag.

Lemarcus backed them out of the driveway. "What's in the bag?"

"A lot of heroin," Austin said. "Enough to last for days. And plenty of clean needles. They're brand new. I also got us a spoon, a box of Q-tips, and a couple of rubber tubes to tie our arms off. We'll have to get some water though, and a cigarette lighter. I guess we'll have to get some camping supplies, too."

"Camping supplies?"

"Yeah, man. I called my dad while I was in there, from someone's burner phone, and he told me to not come home for a couple of days, so I figured you and I can hide out up in the mountains. You cool with that?"

At a stop sign, Lemarcus turned left on Vine Street. "Yeah, man. I'm cool with that. I'll have to stop and get more booze, though. And some cigarettes."

At a camping supplies store on Eisenhower Drive, they bought two sleeping bags, a fast-pitch tent, a can of lighter fluid, and two 4-pack bundles of campfire roasting logs. At the grocery store next door, they bought a case of bottled water and several snacks. At a liquor store down the street, they purchased two half-gallons of whiskey, a six-pack of Bic lighters, and a carton of cigarettes.

Then Austin guided Lemarcus from Eisenhower to the interstate, to Rock Creek Road, to Dry Hill Drive, and to

Marfork Lane. From there, they turned onto an unmarked, two-lane road that corkscrewed up into the mountains. The forest quickly thickened, looming close to the road like impassable walls.

"I ain't never been on this road before," Lemarcus said. He thought the jagged stones sticking out of the earth resembled the bones of half-buried dinosaurs. Occasionally, rutted trails snaked up into the forest from the main road. "Where do those trails go?"

"Remote territory," Austin said. "Savage places where hillbillies and inbred families still cling to the values of the old world."

"Are we still in Warlington?"

"Technically, yes. On the western edge of the city. But those trails go for miles and miles into the forest, leading to some truly fucked-up places."

Lemarcus laughed. "You won't catch my black ass on those trails."

At the top of the mountain, he parked the car in a clearing surrounded by maple trees. "Is this cool?"

Austin nodded. "Works for me."

Lemarcus killed the engine, and they got out.

While Austin set up the tent, Lemarcus cracked open one of the half-gallons and took a few shots of whiskey. He enjoyed panoramic views through the trees: of the city far below to the east and more mountains to the west. There was still plenty of daylight but, to the west, the sun had begun lowering over the mountains.

"It's still too early to start a fire," Lemarcus said.

Finished with setting up the tent, Austin put the sleeping bags inside and zipped it shut. "I'm ready to shoot some heroin," he said.

Lemarcus took a drink. "You go right ahead. I'll pass on that shit." He sat down in the shade of a maple tree.

Austin shrugged. "Suit yourself." From the car, he retrieved the brown paper bag and the vehicle owner's manual from the glove compartment. Removing his jacket, he set it on the ground and joined Lemarcus beneath the maple, with his back against the tree trunk. From the paper bag, he withdrew a baggie of white powder, a hypodermic syringe with a needle attached, and a spoon. Then he withdrew a Q-tip. "Fuck. I forgot to grab some water."

"I'll get you some." Lemarcus got up, grabbed a bottle from the car, and sat back down. "Here you go."

"Thanks." Austin set the bottle on the ground beside him. Unbuttoning his shirt, he pulled his left arm out of its sleeve and tied one of the rubber tubes around his bicep. A blue vein rose. Using the owner's manual as a tray across his lap, he dumped out enough heroin for a hit. He drew some water from the bottle with his syringe and pressed it out into the spoon. After stirring the heroin up with the water in the spoon, he cooked it over a cigarette lighter's flame. Then he drew the heroin from the spoon into the syringe, flicked air out of its tube, and injected himself.

The heroin, evidently, hit him quickly, for Lemarcus watched him lean back against the tree trunk, relax, and smile dreamily. Then his whole body stiffened and went rigid, as if he were having a seizure. He made gurgling sounds when he breathed and started foaming at the mouth. His eyes rolled back in his head. Then his eyes closed, and he stopped breathing with the needle still in his arm.

Lemarcus pulled the needle out and tossed it aside. "Austin!" He grabbed his shoulders and shook him a few times. "Wake up, white boy! Austin! Are you okay?"

There was no response.

Lemarcus checked him for a pulse but didn't find one.

Fuck! Lemarcus thought, freaking out. He knew paramedics often kick-started the hearts of overdose victims with adrenaline, but he also knew that he could not drive Austin to a hospital in time to make a difference.

Not knowing what else to do, Lemarcus drew a fist back and—BOOM—punched him in the chest as hard as he could.

Austin's eyes popped open, but they were misaligned. Not crossed, but splayed outward. One eye was turned far to the left and the other far to the right. He looked crazy.

Brain damage? Lemarcus thought. Irreversible harm?

Lemarcus hit him again, BOOM, right in the chest, and his eyes came back in alignment to stare straight ahead.

"Whoa, man," Austin said. "What happened?"

"You were dead, white boy."

"Dead?"

"Yeah, man. Dead. You overdosed and died. I checked for a pulse, and everything. You were gone, so I punched you in the chest and brought you back."

"How long was I dead?"

"Not long. Maybe a minute or so."

"Damn, dude, I thought I was dreaming. And the dream seemed to last forever."

"What were you dreaming about? Floating above your body, looking down?"

"Nah, man. It's like…I wasn't even here. I was somewhere else, talking to these…things. It was almost like a DMT trip. You ever done DMT?"

Lemarcus took a drink. "Nope. Can't say I have."

"Yeah, man, it's like…whatever those things were, they kept telling me that I didn't need drugs anymore, and I believed them. And I still do. So that's it. I'm not taking drugs anymore. Let me hit that whiskey."

Lemarcus handed him the bottle. Austin took a drink and gave the bottle back.

Then Austin got up, grabbed one of the roasting logs and the lighter fluid from the car, and started a campfire. He proffered the paper bag to Lemarcus. "Sure you don't want this heroin, before I burn it?"

Lemarcus shook his head. "I don't want that shit."

Austin tossed the bag into the flames. Then he sat down next to Lemarcus by the fire. They passed the bottle of whiskey back and forth a couple of times.

"Thanks for saving my life," Austin said.

Lemarcus lit a cigarette. "You owe me one now, motherfucker."

Austin laughed. "Yeah, I suppose that's true. Anyway, you said you graduated from Alcorn State."

"Yep. Six years ago, down in Mississippi."

"What was your major?"

"English lit. I was an English teacher for three years until I lost my job recently."

"No shit? An English teacher. That's cool. Let me ask you a question. Do you have a half-finished novel somewhere that you take out and tinker with from time to time?"

Lemarcus shot him a look. "Yeah, motherfucker. Actually, I do. How did you know that shit?"

"My sister told me that. I'm not a big reader, but she is. She also likes to write, and she once told me that most English teachers have a manuscript they like to take out and play with occasionally."

"How old's your sister?"

"24. Three years younger than me."

"She ever publish anything?"

"No. My sister's not very good. Don't tell her I said that, though. That bitch is fucking crazy."

Lemarcus blew a smoke ring. "I'll keep that in mind. She live with you and the rest of your family in that big house you told me about?"

"Yeah. You've probably heard of us, by the way. Our last name's Winfield."

"Winfield? As in Wesley Winfield?"

"Yep. Wesley's my dad."

"Holy shit! So, you live in that mansion on Holt Mountain? The one that's built into the side of the mountain, and like…crawls all the way up to the top?"

Austin nodded. "That's our house. I told you it was big."

"Big? You can probably see that house from outer space." Finished with his cigarette, Lemarcus flipped it aside. "Let me hit that whiskey."

Austin handed him the bottle. Lemarcus took a drink and gave it back.

"From what I hear," Lemarcus said, "your father basically owns the whole city of Warlington."

Austin shrugged. "Something like that. His great-grandfather was one of the original coal barons. Founded the Winfield Mining Corporation, back in the day. The company's been passed down through generations, of course, but my grandfather branched out into organized crime, for some reason. I think he simply enjoyed breaking the law. And then my dad... Well, let's just say he's taken the whole organized-crime thing farther than his dad could have imagined. I'm sure you've heard some stories."

Lemarcus nodded. "Oh, yes. Definitely. From what I've heard, your father's one of the most ruthless motherfuckers on planet Earth. I've been hearing stories about Wesley my entire life. Some people say he's a vampire. Others say he's a demon. Some actually claim he's the devil himself."

Austin took a drink. "Just rumors. None of those stories are true. But he does like to dabble in the dark arts and black magic from time to time."

"What were you doing in the psych ward, anyway?" Lemarcus asked.

"Got arrested for DUI. I mean, I get stopped driving intoxicated all the time, but I always just give the cops a few grand or whatever cash I have on me, and they let me go. This time, however, I got stopped at a roadblock, a random DUI checkpoint with cops all over the place and none of them were willing to take a bribe in front of fellow officers."

"And they sent you to the psych ward, instead of jail?"

"No, man. They took me to jail but, when they were processing me, one of the questions they asked was if I was suicidal, and I said yes."

"You're suicidal?" Lemarcus asked.

"Nah, dude. I just said that to avoid going to gen pop. I have anger issues, man, and knew if they put me with the other inmates, I probably would have killed someone, and then it would have been a lot harder to get out. So, they put me in isolation, on suicide watch, and then my dad pulled some strings while I was under observation and got me transferred to the psych ward. He could have gotten me out at any time, of course, but he left me in there to get sober, because he hates that I take drugs. But then that shit-talking orderly pissed me off, so I killed him, and here we are."

"Sounds like your dad has a heart after all," Lemarcus said. "I mean, leaving you locked up to get sober must mean that he loves you."

Austin took a drink. "Oh, yes. Definitely. He's a ruthless son of a bitch, but there's no doubt that he loves me and my sister. And he's gonna like you, too, after he finds out that I died and you brought me back to life."

Lemarcus cracked a grin. "Does that mean you're gonna take me home to meet your family?"

Austin laughed. "Dude, where the fuck else you gonna go? If you come and work with me, for my dad, you'll have plenty of money, a place to live inside the mansion, and a new ID. Be a way to wipe the slate clean, so to speak. But it's totally up to you, of course."

"Hell yeah, white boy. That sounds good, actually. Let me hit that whiskey."

They drank until the sun set and ate a few candy bars. The first stars of twilight started sparkling.

They resumed drinking, and the sky turned black.

To Lemarcus, the city below the mountains resembled something he could crush between his fingers or beneath his feet. He lit a cigarette and poked their campfire with a stick, prodding its embers into a spray of sparks that rose toward the stars. "Let me ask you a question, white boy. You got kids?"

"No. Not anymore."

"Whatchu mean?"

"I had a wife and a daughter," Austin said, "but they're both dead."

"Damn, dude! What the fuck happened?"

"Car crash. Two years ago. Sadie was 25. Nova was 5."

"Sorry to hear that, man. That is messed up."

Austin took a drink. "Yeah, man. It's crazy how fast that rug can get yanked out from beneath your feet. A drunk driver crossed center line and hit them head-on, doing 75. Sadie and Nova died instantly. That piece of shit who hit them walked away unscathed."

"Did you kill that motherfucker?"

"Yep. Took him in the woods, tied him to a tree, and skinned him alive. Before I dropped his corpse down a mineshaft, I picked up the 57 capsules of smelling salts I had used to keep him awake."

Lemarcus nodded. "Good for you. Let me hit that whiskey."

Austin handed him the bottle.

"My daughter's 8," Lemarcus said. "Her name's Makayla. Right now, she's with her bitch-ass mom, Shanice. I wanna kill Shanice and take Makayla with me."

"I don't blame you, dude. Didn't you say Shanice had you arrested, for beating her up, even though you never touched her?"

"Yep. She had her brother and her brother's boyfriend beat her up, then told the police it was me. When the police got there, her brother and his boyfriend told the police they saw me do it. I wanna kill those motherfuckers, too."

"We can do that," Austin said. "Where does her brother and his boyfriend live?"

Lemarcus shrugged. "Last I heard, they were staying at my house."

"Your house?"

"Yep. After Shanice had me arrested, she put a restraining order against me, so I wasn't even allowed to go home. She let her brother and his boyfriend move in, supposedly for 'protection.' Now all three of them stay wasted on drugs with my daughter in the house while I'm homeless. The whole thing's crazy."

"You're not homeless," Austin said. "You and your daughter can come and live with my family, on Holt Mountain. It's gonna be okay. We'll go kill your wife and her piece-of-shit brother and his boyfriend tomorrow, after we sober up."

Lemarcus lit a cigarette. "Cool."

They drank until the bottle was empty, then crawled into their sleeping bags inside the tent and went to sleep.

CH. 6

Rick discovered long ago that it wasn't easy for him meeting women. Some dudes could just walk up to chicks and start talking to them about anything, but he couldn't do it. He had to work up his courage with a few beers or a couple of whiskeys, had to sit at a table or the bar for a while and look them over, try to find one who looked like she wouldn't shoot him down in flames. This often meant choosing one by herself, and tonight, on a Saturday in a tavern just outside the city limits, one sitting at a table across the room caught his eye.

Long, blonde hair cascaded from beneath a baseball cap on her head. She wore a blue tank top and light-blue denim pants. She took a sip from a glass of clear liquid, looking straight at him.

Grabbing his beer, Rick rose from his barstool and approached her. "Hello," he said when he stopped in front of her table. Thankfully, the volume of the music was not so loud that he had to shout.

She smiled but didn't say anything.

Then he noticed the duffel bag hanging from one shoulder and the suitcase on the floor next to her feet. "You're not from around here, are you?"

"Nope."

"You traveling?"

She shrugged. "Something like that."

"Where ya from?"

"Around."

"Around?"

"Yep. Around the way. I mean, what's it matter anyway? Why do you give a fuck where I'm from?"

He laughed. "I don't, really. It was just something to say. I never know what to say around pretty girls."

She smiled again. "You think I'm pretty?"

"Yeah. Wanna dance?"

She cocked her head. "That's what you're asking me? If I would like to dance with you?"

"Yeah. Come on. It'll be fun."

She shook her head. "No, thank you."

"Oh, come on. I don't bite."

She shook her head again. "No, thanks. I don't dance with strangers. Actually, I don't dance with anyone. But we can talk, if you want to. Would you like to talk with me?"

"Sure!" He pulled a chair back, sat down, and sipped his beer. "I'm Rick, by the way."

She sipped her drink. "Rick. Nice name. Reminds me of Crick."

"Crick?"

"Yes. Francis Crick. Do you know who that was?"

Rick shook his head. "No idea."

"British molecular biologist and neuroscientist. Back in the 1950s, he and another scientist—James Watson—transformed our understanding of the nature of life when they illuminated the chemical structure and information-bearing properties of DNA. Since then, we've learned that all living things depend upon digital information that is stored in a four-character code embedded in the twisting figure of a double helix."

Rick sipped his beer. "What's your name?"

"Britney."

"You seem pretty smart. Did you go to college, or something?"

"No, but I do like to read. I've been reading for as long as I can remember."

"You sound like you're from Texas, or somewhere."

She laughed. "We're all from somewhere, Rick. But no, I'm not from Texas. Right now, I guess you could say I'm just a drifter."

"Is that what you're doing? Just passing through?"

Britney finished her drink. "Yep. Just passing through. You know any hotels around this place?"

"Pioneer Motel." Rick finished his beer. "About a mile up the road, on the highway. You need a ride?"

"Sure! That would be great!" She grabbed her suitcase and rose from the table.

His car was parked in front of the building. Britney put her suitcase in the back, then climbed in the passenger's side. While he drove her to the motel, she rambled on about things that made zero sense to Rick, but he pretended to know what she was talking about.

When they reached the motel, a ranch-style building with a long row of rooms facing the lot, Rick parked in front of the office and killed the engine. The office was lit up. According to the sign, vacancy was available. He saw a bored-looking young man with a blue mohawk at the front desk through the office window.

Britney put a hand on his leg. "I have some vodka in my duffel bag. Wanna help me drink it?"

"Absolutely," Rick replied, feeling a rush of blood to his penis. "I'd be happy to."

She smiled. "I'll go get a room. Be right back." Britney went inside the office. Less than five minutes later, she got back in the car. "Since checkout time's at 11, I booked the room for two days."

Rick moved the car in front of her room. They got out and went inside.

There were two queen-sized beds in the room.

Rick, holding Britney's suitcase, said, "You gonna let me crash here? If I get too drunk to drive?"

"Sure! Just set that suitcase on the bed nearest the bathroom."

Rick did. "Fucker's heavy. What do you have in this thing, anyway? Goddamn dumbbells, or something?"

Britney laughed. "No, not dumbbells. Guns and ammo, mostly."

"Seriously?"

"Yep." She set her duffel bag on the bed nearest the window.

"I love guns," Rick said. "Mind if I take a look?"

"Not at all." She retrieved a bottle of vodka from her duffel bag and took a drink. "Knock yourself out."

Rick opened the suitcase, and his eyes widened. Then he whistled at the sight of the sawed-off shotgun, numerous handguns, and the disassembled AR-15. Also within the suitcase were several knives, sound suppressors for pistols, and spare magazines loaded with hollow-point rounds in various calibers. "Damn, girl. You planning on going to war, or some shit?"

She laughed again, but this time, Rick heard no mirth. This time, he heard a maniacal cackle.

"No," Britney said. "I'm not planning on going to war. But I live in accordance with an old Chinese proverb: It's better to be a warrior in a garden, than a gardener in a war." She handed him the bottle, and he took a drink. Then she pulled a pistol from her duffel bag and aimed it at his face. "Close the suitcase," she said.

He did.

"Now go sit down on one of those chairs by the window."

He did, and Britney sat on the other chair with the gun still aimed at his face.

Staring into the pistol's black muzzle, Rick knew it was either a .380 or a 9mm. "What the hell's your function, anyway?" he asked her.

"I have many. Let me hit that vodka."

He pushed the bottle across the table, and she took a drink, still aiming the gun at his face. Then she took another drink and slid the bottle back.

Her finger was on the trigger and Rick knew, if he made one wrong move, his brains would go flying out the back of his head. "Is this a robbery?" he asked. "I mean, I don't have much money, but you're welcome to what I have."

Resting her elbow on the table, she lowered the gun but kept it aimed at his chest. "I don't need your money, trust me. I'm likely one of the richest people you'll ever meet."

"Then where's your car? Why are you on foot? And what were you doing at a bar in North Carolina with a suitcase full of guns and ammunition?"

"I've been traveling," Britney said, "for 27 days. I've killed 27 people in 27 states."

"Is that right?"

She smiled. "It could be."

"So, what are you? An assassin? A serial killer? A vigilante?"

"Maybe I'm all those things. Or none of those things. Or all those things and more. Maybe my whole family's a shadow society. Let me hit that vodka."

He pushed the bottle across the table. She took a drink and slid the bottle back.

"Some people can get away with anything," Britney said. "Like my family. We don't play by the rules. We make our own rules as we go and play by those."

"And what exactly are those rules?"

"They're complicated. You'd never understand."

Rick took a drink. "Are you going to kill me?"

Rising from her chair, she grabbed the front of his shirt and put the gun to his head. "That depends."

"On what?"

"On whether or not you can fuck me with a gun to your head."

Rick smiled. "I think I can manage."

With the muzzle to his forehead, she lowered her left hand and clutched his penis, which was stiff. "You're hard as a rock."

He nodded.

"Does the danger turn you on?"

Rick felt his temperature rise. "I don't know, but something about you definitely turns me on."

She pulled him to the bed next to the table, the one on which her duffel bag still sat, and kicked off her shoes. Rick followed suit. Then, while Britney pressed the muzzle to his temple, he pulled her pants off, then his own. He could feel his cock throbbing with his heartbeat.

She hiked a leg up and put it over his shoulder. "Fuck me with this gun to your head, and I just might let you live."

As he thrust himself inside her, she grabbed the back of his neck with her free hand, never letting the other move the gun from his head.

He could not believe how hot and wet she was.

"Harder," Britney insisted, and he obliged her, trying not to come too fast.

To distract himself, he bit down on his tongue until he tasted blood.

"Don't stop," she told him. "I'm gonna come."

He tried counting down from a hundred, but her moans broke his concentration, and he lost count.

Her whole body quaked, and her vagina soaked his penis as she came, which sent him over the edge, and he exploded. He saw bright lights, colors, and felt as if his body had blown itself apart, sending his brain into the cosmos, blazing like a star in the dark.

Then he drifted back down to the bed, on top of Britney, as she held the gun to his head.

"I need a drink," Britney said.

"Me too."

They got up, put their pants back on, and took a few shots of vodka on the bed.

"I wanna hear more about your family," Rick said. "And those rules you told me I wouldn't understand."

Britney no longer held the gun. She had set it atop the duffel bag to her right. Rick sat to her left on the edge of the bed. "There's a dungeon in our mansion," Britney said.

"A dungeon?"

"Yes. My great-great-grandfather practiced sorcery and black magic. He was also quite sadistic and enjoyed torturing people. He worshipped ancient gods of pain and suffering and sacrificed people in the dungeon as offerings to the merciless gods he adored."

Rick took a drink. "I bet he was a lot of fun at parties."

"He was a great writer, too. We keep his manuscripts in a safe in the library. As a matter of fact, my family still practices his teachings to this day."

"Is that right?"

"Yes. He was a very spiritual man. There was no doubt in his mind that consciousness survives death, and his philosophy was that life is all about pain. The more pain a person receives in this life, the greater their rewards in the next. And the more pain a person delivers to others in this life, the greater their chances of being a god in the next. Let me hit that vodka."

He handed her the bottle. "So, your whole family tortures people to death?"

"Yes. Well, everyone except my brother. He's fucked up, just not as fucked up as the rest of us. But we still love him."

Rick rose from the bed. "I need to piss."

He went into the bathroom and closed the door. When he came back out, Britney stood facing him with the pistol aimed at his chest, and he noticed that she had attached one of the suppressors to the end of its barrel.

"You were never afraid?" Britney asked. "Even with the gun to your head?"

"No. It's just death. It's just nonexistence."

"You don't believe in life after death?"

"No. There is no other side."

From six feet away, he watched her raise the gun from his chest to his face.

"You're wrong," she said. "There is another side. That's why I do what I do. I want to be a goddess in the afterlife."

Those were the last words he heard.

Britney pulled the trigger and shot him through the face. She watched his head break apart and veer off in different directions, a wash of blood and brain splashing against the walls and into the bathroom behind him. He was dead before he dropped straight down.

She unscrewed the silencer, shoved it beneath her duffel bag, and tucked the pistol into the back of her jeans.

Then she left the room and walked back to the front office. The receptionist with a blue mohawk looked up from his phone.

"Hi," Britney said. "Sorry to bother you again, but is there any way I can get a tube of toothpaste?"

"Sure! Do you need a toothbrush, too?"

"No, I have a toothbrush. Just realized that I'm completely out of toothpaste."

"No problem. Be right back." He got up, walked off, and then returned with a tube of toothpaste. "Here you go."

"Thanks!"

He smiled. "My pleasure."

Britney turned to leave, but then turned back around. "Also, would you please let housekeeping know that I won't need my room cleaned in the morning? I'm working on a book, and I usually write all night, so end up sleeping late."

"Sure! I'll let them know. What kinda book you writing?"

"A fucked-up book," Britney said.

He laughed. "Hell yeah! Sounds like my kind of book!"

Britney tipped her cap and winked. "See you around."

CH. 7

Lemarcus woke at sunrise on the mountain. He felt great but was thirsty and his mouth tasted awful. He crawled from his sleeping bag, stepped out of the tent, and saw that Austin had already opened their second half-gallon of whiskey.

Sitting cross-legged on the ground, Austin clutched the bottle next to the ashes of their campfire.

"Damn, white boy. You already drinking?"

Austin offered the bottle. "You want a shot?"

"Not yet. I'm thirsty as a motherfucker."

From the dead woman's car, Lemarcus grabbed two bottles of water and chugged them both. Then he sat on the ground to Austin's right.

Austin handed him the bottle.

Lemarcus took a drink. "Damn, that hits the spot." He took two more drinks and gave the bottle back. "We still gonna kill my wife's brother today?"

Austin nodded. "Yeah, dude. Him and his piece-of-shit boyfriend. What are their names again?"

"Her brother's name is Darius, and his boyfriend's name is Jayden."

Austin took a drink. "Darius and Jayden. And they're staying at your old house?"

Lemarcus shrugged. "Far as I know."

"And where exactly is your house?"

"Myers Avenue. You know where that's at?"

"Yeah, man. Over on the east side."

Lemarcus looked at the car. "You think we should switch license plates, when we get back down to town?"

"I was thinking about that earlier," Austin said. "And I don't think we should. Not today, anyway. Maybe tomorrow. I mean, today's Sunday, so we have that in our favor. The owner of the car, whatever the fuck her name was, no one should notice her missing until tomorrow."

Lemarcus nodded. "Yeah, you're probably right."

"But what about these clothes?" Austin asked. "You think we'll look conspicuous, in business attire on a Sunday?"

Lemarcus shook his head. "Nah, man. Like you said, this is Sunday. We'll just look like we're on our way to church, or some shit. Let me hit that whiskey."

Austin handed him the bottle.

Lemarcus took a drink and gave the bottle back. "Wish we had some mouthwash. Something besides this whiskey to kill the morning breath."

"Let's go to Walmart," Austin said. "You can wait in the car while I grab some mouthwash and deodorant."

Lemarcus glanced at the tent. "We just gonna leave our stuff here?"

"Yeah, man. It's just a cheap-ass tent and a couple of sleeping bags. Ain't nobody gonna mess with our stuff."

"What if someone's in the tent, though, when we get back?"

Austin held up his gun. "Then we'll ask them to leave."

"Cool," Lemarcus said.

When they got to the Walmart down the mountain, Austin went inside, then got back in the car ten minutes later. Each rinsed with Scope and spat mouthwash out the window. They put on deodorant and headed across town to Myers Avenue.

"There's my house," Lemarcus said, pointing at his one-story home as he drove past. "Her brother's there, but I don't see Shanice's car in the driveway." He parked half a block up the street and killed the engine. According to the dashboard clock, the time was **7:36 AM**.

"Early as hell," Austin said. "What are their names again?"

"Her brother's name is Darius, and his boyfriend's name is Jayden. They're probably still asleep."

"You got an alarm system on that house?"

Lemarcus shook his head. "Nah, man. There ain't no alarm system on that house."

"Is there a deadbolt lock on the front door?"

"Nope. Not unless they put one on since the restraining order, which I seriously doubt."

Austin reached down and picked up the dead orderly's wallet, which had still been on the floorboard. From the wallet, he withdrew the orderly's driver's license and a credit card. "I can pick the lock with one of these, as long as the slant of the latch is facing me. Do you know if it is?"

"I have no idea."

"Well, as long as the hinges are on the inside of the door, we're good to go. Do you know if they are?"

"Man, I ain't never paid attention to the goddamn hinges. And how do you know so much about picking a lock anyway, since your family has so much money?"

Austin laughed. "Dude, working for my dad all these years…you would not believe some of the crimes I've committed. But you'll see as soon as you start working for him."

Lemarcus shrugged. "Whatever. Let's do this shit."

They got out and walked half a block down the street to Lemarcus's house.

On the front porch, Lemarcus put a finger to his lips, listening. "I don't think Makayla's here," he whispered. "I mean, I know Shanice's car ain't here, but I don't think Makayla's here either. If she was, we'd probably hear some video games or some cartoons. She gets up early." He drew his gun. "Maybe Darius and Jayden can tell us where they are."

"Look," Austin whispered, pointing at the door. "We're in luck. The hinges are on the opposite side."

Austin picked the lock, drew his gun, then opened the door. "After you."

Lemarcus stepped inside. Austin followed.

Lemarcus closed the door and locked it. He cast his gaze around the living room, which was filthier than he had ever seen it. He shook his head. "This place looks like a fucking pigsty."

He checked Makayla's room first but found it empty. Next, he checked the master bedroom, but it was empty, too.

Then he found Darius and Jayden side-by-side in the spare bedroom, sound asleep.

"Rise and shine, sleepyheads," Lemarcus said.

Darius opened his eyes, but Jayden never even stirred.

"Where's Shanice?" Lemarcus asked, pointing his gun at Darius. "And where the fuck's my daughter?"

Darius rubbed his eyes. "Lemarcus? What the fuck are you doing here?"

Lemarcus looked at Austin, who entered the room alongside him and nodded. "Kill his bitch."

Austin raised his gun and shot Jayden through the head while he slept. Blood, pieces of brain, and skull fragments hit Darius in the face.

"Jesus fucking Christ!" Darius said.

Lemarcus lowered his gun and blew off one of Darius's kneecaps. "Tell me where Shanice is! And my daughter! Or I'll blow your fucking balls off!"

"They at Tremaine's place, man!" Darius shrieked.

"Tremaine's place? You talkin' about Tremaine Johnson, over on Temple Street?"

Darius nodded, grimacing and clutching his ruined knee. "Yeah, man. Shanice and Makayla's been stayin' there about two weeks."

Lemarcus raised the gun. "Thank you very much." Then he shot Darius through the head.

"Let's get the fuck outta here," Austin said.

CH. 8

"I'm stopping here," Mason said from behind the steering wheel. They were traveling back to New Jersey after visiting Carol's parents in southern Georgia. He had seen a sign for the Pioneer Motel on the highway a few miles back and, now that they had arrived, Carol opened her eyes next to him on the passenger's side.

"Are we still in South Carolina?" she asked.

"No. You've been asleep for like…two hours. We're in North Carolina now, and I'm not driving anymore. I'm ready for a beer and a cigarette, in that order."

Behind them, Carol's 10-year-old son Henry said, "I'm hungry."

Little bastard's always hungry, Mason thought. He released the steering wheel and cracked his knuckles. "I'll order a pizza after I get us a room."

"That woman on the porch looks like a prostitute," Carol said.

Mason had already been checking out the young woman as she sat on an outdoor chair in front of the office, smoking a cigarette. Dressed in blue jeans and a tank top, she had long, blonde hair and wore a baseball cap cocked sideways.

"She probably just works here," Mason said. Leaving the engine running, he got out of the car, closed his door, and stepped up onto the porch.

The young woman flashed him a grin. "Hi! I'm Britney. How may I help you?"

He returned her smile. "I'm Mason. I need a room."

"Two beds? One for you and your wife, and one for your son?"

Mason looked behind him to make sure Carol's window was still up, so she couldn't hear what he was about to say. Then he told Britney, "He's not my son. And she's not my wife. She's just my girlfriend."

Still smiling, Britney nodded. "I see. And I don't work here, by the way. I'm just passing through. But I'd be happy to help you in other ways, if you can get away from your girlfriend long enough."

"What room you staying in?"

"I can't tell you that," Britney said. "But don't worry. If you step outside, I'll see you."

Mason knew that was probably true, as the Pioneer was a park-by-the-door motel with a single-story strip of rooms facing the lot. He winked. "I'll see what I can do."

Then he went inside the front office, where he paid a young man with a blue mohawk for a two-bed room.

The man gave him a keycard. "Enjoy your stay. If you need anything, just give me a call here at the front desk."

When Mason stepped outside, he saw that Britney had lit another cigarette.

"Perhaps I'll see you around," she said.

"Maybe so."

He returned to the car, parked in front of their room, unloaded their luggage, and they went inside.

"This place is a dump," Carol said. She sat on the bed nearest the window.

Mason set their luggage on the floor. "It's got four walls and a roof. It's all we need."

Henry found the remote to the TV, sat down on the bed nearest the bathroom, and began flicking through channels. "I'm hungry. Can we order a pizza now?"

"Hold your horses," Mason said. "I wanna drink a few beers first." He walked outside and popped his trunk. He looked toward the office, but no longer saw Britney sitting on the porch. He grabbed his case of beer and went back inside.

Henry had found a cartoon about dinosaurs and was watching that.

Carol sat, looking down at her phone. "Did they give you a Wi-Fi password? At the front desk?"

"Nope." Mason sat down at the table by the window, cracked open a beer, and started chugging.

"Is it written on the keycard sleeve?" Carol asked.

"There was no keycard sleeve. Just a keycard."

"Jesus Christ," Carol said, exasperated. "This place may not even have free Wi-Fi."

Mason finished his beer and opened another one. "Can you stop bitching for five goddamn seconds?"

"Fine!" Carol got up, went into the bathroom, and slammed the door.

The clerk with a blue mohawk looked up from his phone and smiled when Britney stepped into the office. "Hi!" he said. "How's your book coming along?"

"Great! I'm having a lot of fun with it. And I don't know if I told you this, but I absolutely love your punk-rock hair."

"Thanks! I play bass in a punk band called The Ravagers. I'm Jude, by the way."

"Nice name! I'm Britney."

Jude cocked his head. "Britney? That's not the name you checked in under."

"No, it's not. I always check in under a different name. I use a lot of aliases and pseudonyms. I've had some problems with stalkers in the past."

"Know what you mean," Jude said. "Believe it or not, I've had a few stalkers, too."

"Because of your music?"

"Yep. And we're not even famous. Can you imagine what celebrities go through?"

"There's definitely some weird people out there." From her duffel bag, she retrieved one of the joints she had rolled earlier and held it up. "Do you smoke weed?"

He smiled. "Absolutely."

"You wanna smoke some weed with me?"

"Definitely! I can lock the office and we can go smoke it in your room, if you want."

Britney shook her head. She had dragged Rick's corpse into the bathroom, but his blood was still splattered all over the walls. "Nah, I've been cooped up in my room, writing. Is there somewhere else we can smoke it?"

"Sure!" Jude walked over to the front entrance and turned the sign **CLOSED**. Then he locked the door and led her outside through a side door. They crossed an alcove between the rooms and the motel office, where the ice and vending machines were, and Britney followed him into a stockroom. Jude closed the door and locked it.

Britney sat on the floor next to a crate of toilet paper and lit the joint. He joined her on the floor, sitting cross-legged to her left, and she handed him the joint. "Go ahead and hit it a few times," she told him. "I'm already high. You need to catch up."

While Jude held some pot smoke in his lungs, Britney retrieved a hypodermic syringe from her duffel bag, slammed the needle into his thigh through his pants, and pressed the plunger.

It took him a few seconds to react to what she had done. Then he said, "What the fuck was that?"

"Rocuronium," she told him. "It's good stuff. You'll see."

"Bitch, I've never even heard of that shit! And I don't goddamn shoot up drugs, anyway!"

She chopped him in the throat with the side of her hand, yanked him forward, and shoved his face onto the floor.

While he choked and wheezed for air, she hit the joint a couple times, and then stubbed it out.

Moments later, the paralytic took effect, and he stopped moving.

Britney rolled him over, flat onto his back. As he stared up at her, horrified, she smiled. He was able to blink, and his chest rose and fell as he breathed, but he otherwise lay motionless.

She put the syringe and joint back in her duffel bag. Then she put on a pair of gloves.

"I have a large family," Britney said. "Cousins, aunts, uncles, my mom and dad, my brother—we all live in one big, happy home. I like to travel a lot though, and certain members of my family like me to bring souvenirs when I return. I'm not talking about T-shirts, hats, and postcards, however. I'm talking about scalps. I'm talking about penises and testicles. I'm talking about ears, lips, and eyeballs. That's why there's a jar of formaldehyde in my suitcase, back in my room."

She got up, stripped naked, but left the gloves on.

"Hell, I got one uncle who loves when I bring him the skulls of small children. But enough of that. Right now, it's time to decide which parts of you are worth taking home to my family."

She removed his clothes. In his wallet, she found a keycard she knew was a master key to the motel rooms and put it in her duffel bag.

Then she withdrew a sharp knife and a blowtorch.

While Mason drank beer at the table by the window, Carol and Henry fell asleep on their separate beds. Thank fucking God, Mason thought. Peace at last.

On the TV screen, animated dinosaurs spoke English while crossing a charred wasteland.

Mason finished his beer. Then he stepped outside to smoke a cigarette. After he smoked it, he lit another one, giving Britney plenty of time to see him. He even walked up and down the sidewalk a couple times, wondering which room she was in. There weren't many people staying at the motel. Besides his own, he counted four vehicles in the parking lot. It's still early, Mason thought. More travelers will stop here later, after the sun sets.

He went back inside and opened another beer.

Finished with Jude, Britney scrubbed his blood off her hands at a sink with a rag and liquid soap in the stockroom. Then she put her clothes back on, grabbed her duffel bag, and stepped outside. She knew that Jude's car was parked on the side of the building. One of those cars belonged to the dead man in her bathroom who drove her here. Another belonged to Mason—but she was saving him, his girlfriend, and the little boy for last.

So, Britney thought, that means two other rooms are currently occupied.

Drawing the silencer-fitted pistol from her duffel bag, she went to the nearest door in front of which a vehicle was parked. Moans of sexual pleasure emanated from the room. Using her master key, she opened the door and stepped inside with her gun up.

On the lone, queen-sized bed, a man lay flat on his back. A woman lay on her hands and knees atop him with his penis in her mouth. The man licked her vagina from behind.

Britney shot the woman through the head, then executed the man two seconds later. The suppressor had reduced the gunfire to a whisper, and both victims voided their bowels upon their deaths.

In the next room Britney entered, a Mexican sat on the bed, watching TV. He looked at Britney in complete surprise before she shot him in the face, leaving a wash of blood across the wall above the headboard.

She could hear water running in the bathroom. Seconds later, she heard the water shut off, followed by the shower curtain swishing open. Then a nude Mexican woman with a towel around her head came out of the bathroom. She stopped dead in her tracks when she saw Britney aiming a gun at her face. Her eyes widened at the sight of the dead man on the bed, but she didn't scream.

"Oh my," Britney said. "You have two of the prettiest eyes I've ever seen."

The woman said nothing.

"My mother will love them," Britney added.

She shot the woman through the heart, then retrieved a knife from her duffel bag to remove the woman's eyes.

After a few more beers, Mason stepped outside to smoke a cigarette. To the west, the sun was starting to lower, but still no other cars had arrived in the parking lot. He glanced toward the office, looking for Britney, then walked up and down the sidewalk while he smoked. If Britney was looking for him, he didn't see her.

Finished smoking, he went back inside the room, where Carol and Henry were both awake.

"I'm hungry," Henry said.

Mason opened a beer.

Carol said, "There's no menus in here. I already checked. There's not even a phone book. What kind of motel doesn't have menus for nearby restaurants in their rooms?"

"Call the front desk," Mason said. "Dude with a mohawk told me to call the front desk if we need anything."

Carol called the front desk, but no one answered.

"I'll just walk up there and talk to him," Mason said. "See if he has any menus."

He took off walking, taking his can of Pabst Blue Ribbon with him. When he reached the office, the sign on the door said **CLOSED**. Peering through the glass, he saw that the man with a mohawk was no longer behind the desk.

Great, Mason thought. Maybe he's in the bathroom or taking a dinner break. Nonetheless, locking the front office of a motel this early in the evening seemed to Mason like a good way to lose your job.

He turned and then Britney popped out of an alcove between the rooms and the motel office.

"There you are!" she said, smiling. "I've been looking for you."

"Is that right?"

"Yes." She took his hand and led him into the alcove, where the ice and vending machines were, then opened a door and pulled him into a stockroom.

She kissed him on the mouth while closing and locking the door—then Mason saw the man with a mohawk lying dead on the stockroom floor. The corpse was naked. Burns and cuts covered the flesh from head to toe. The genitals were missing; the groin had been reduced to a gaping, black-and-red hole.

"What are their names?" Britney asked.

Mason turned around, surprised to see her pointing a pistol at his face. "Huh?"

"Their names! Your girlfriend and her little boy! What are their goddamn names?"

"Carol and Henry," Mason said, thinking, *This bitch is fucking insane.*

Britney pulled the trigger, and Mason thought no more.

While his mother was in the bathroom, Henry sat on his bed, watching TV, when a woman—the same woman his mother had said looked like a prostitute earlier—entered the room and closed the door behind her. She didn't look like a prostitute to Henry; he thought she looked more like a movie star. He had never actually seen a prostitute, but he had always envisioned them as disease-ridden creatures of the night with dirty skin, greasy hair, and rotting teeth.

This gorgeous blonde woman, however, in blue jeans and a tank top, seemed more like a Hollywood starlet trying to hide from paparazzi beneath the baseball cap on her head. When she smiled, he thought her white teeth would have looked right at home in a toothpaste commercial.

"Hi, Henry! Is your mother in the bathroom?"

He nodded, assuming that Mason must have told this woman his name.

She approached him and extended a hand. "I'm Britney. It's great to meet you."

Henry shook her hand, and saw her eyes widen as soon as she touched his flesh.

"Oh my," she said. "You have the most beautiful hands I've ever seen. My mother will love them."

The bathroom door opened, and Henry's mother stepped into the room. She took one look at Britney, and her whole demeanor changed. "What are you doing in here?" she asked. "Where's Mason?"

Britney pulled a gun from behind her back and raised it. "Bitch, you don't have anything that even warrants preservation."

Then Henry watched her shoot his mother five times in the chest. The shots only made soft popping sounds, but Henry knew his mother was dead before she thudded to the floor.

Screaming, he bolted for the door, but Britney grabbed a fistful of his hair and slammed him onto the other bed.

"Shut up!" she told him. "You sound like a little bitch!" She clubbed him alongside the head with her pistol, and then hit him again. And again. And again.

The last thing he saw before consciousness faded was Britney pulling a hacksaw out of her duffel bag.

CH. 9

After killing his wife's brother and her brother's boyfriend, Lemarcus drove Austin back to their tent atop the mountain to kill some time and drink some more whiskey. Austin built a campfire and they sat on the ground in front of the tent to smoke cigarettes, awaiting nightfall.

"I'm looking forward to seeing Makayla," Lemarcus said. "And I know she'll be glad to see me, too. She always was a daddy's girl."

"Is that right?"

"Yep. I mean, I know she loves her mother, but Makayla's not stupid. She's only eight years old, but she knows her mom's a piece of fucking shit."

Austin nodded, but said nothing, just stared into the flames, and Lemarcus figured he was probably thinking of the wife and daughter he lost in a car crash two years ago.

Finished with his cigarette, Lemarcus flipped it to the left, the direction in which the lowering sun glowed red. To the east, the sky was purple, vast, and sparkling with the first stars of twilight. "Let me hit that whiskey."

Austin handed him the bottle.

Lemarcus took a drink and gave the bottle back. "You're a good-looking motherfucker, white boy. Is your sister good-looking, too?"

Austin took a drink. "Yeah, man. My sister's a fucking knockout."

"Does she fuck black dudes?"

Austin shot him a look. "Dude, she'll fuck anything. But trust me, you don't wanna get involved with my sister. That bitch is crazier than we are."

"Yeah, but you said she likes to read and write. And I'm a fucking English major. We probably have a bunch of shit in common."

Austin shrugged. "Maybe so. She's definitely an alcoholic, just like you."

Lemarcus laughed. "White boy, you're a goddamn alcoholic, too."

Austin shook his head. "Nope. I'm just a recovering drug addict who likes to drink."

"Whatever." Lemarcus lit a cigarette. "Anyway, Makayla loves to read, too. I taught her how to read before she started kindergarten and now she basically reads like an adult."

"At eight years of age?"

"Yeah, man. She's very precocious."

Austin took a drink. "What the fuck's 'precocious' mean?"

"Unusually advanced, especially mentally. It means she's smart for her age. She was reading Stephen King and Dean Koontz when she was six."

"Seriously?"

"Yep. I'm not sure how much of it she actually understood but, by God, she was reading the shit. Does your sister have a lot of books?"

"Yeah, man. Quite a bit, actually."

"Cool," Lemarcus said. "Maybe she can loan Makayla some books from time to time. And maybe she can help me out with babysitting and stuff. You know, when you and I are out doing gangster shit for your father."

Austin nodded. "Sure. My sister's great with kids. But first, we actually have to go get your daughter."

"I know." Lemarcus looked at the sky. "We'll kill Shanice in about an hour or so, after it's dark. Let me hit that whiskey."

Austin handed him the bottle.

In her filthy bedroom on the second floor of Tremaine Johnson's crowded house on Temple Street, Makayla sat on the floor and ignored the scattering cockroaches, focused instead on the dirty spoon in front of her. She preferred to sit on the floor because bad men came into her room at night and made her do terrible things on the bed. Therefore, she stayed off the bed as much as possible.

She often saw her mom peeking through the crack in the door, watching the bad men do the awful things to her. Her mother never looked away until it was over, and then she would turn and walk off down the hall.

By staring at the spoon, Makayla was trying to develop telekinesis, the ability to move objects with her mind. While there was no scientific proof that telekinesis existed, there was no proof that it *didn't* exist, either.

She became fascinated with psychic abilities after reading about Charlie McGee's pyrokinetic ability to start fires with her mind in Stephen King's *Firestarter*. At eight years of age, Makayla's favorite books were those written by Stephen King and Dean Koontz decades before, books her father had given her from his own library—before her mother had him locked away. She missed her father terribly, and wished she could start fires with her mind like Charlie McGee, in which case she would burn her mother alive.

But first she had to learn to bend a spoon…

Her mother entered the room and set a paper plate next to her on the floor. On the plate was a sandwich surrounded by potato chips. Next to the plate she set a can of generic cola. "That's all you're gettin' today. It's all I can afford. So, ya best be eatin' your food before the roaches do."

Her mother left the room.

Makayla kept her focus on the spoon.

"That's it," Lemarcus said, behind the steering wheel, pointing at Tremaine Johnson's two-story house on Temple Street. "And there's Shanice's car in the driveway."

"There's a shitload of cars in that driveway," Austin said. He drew his Glock, ejected the magazine, inspected it, and then locked it back in place.

"We'll park down the street. He always has a houseful of people." Beyond the windshield, the sky was dark. The dashboard clock showed **10:17 PM**.

They parked and walked toward the house. Tremaine's party poured onto the front porch, the stairs, the yard, the sidewalk, and the street. People—mostly black dudes and white chicks in their twenties—drank, smoked, laughed, and conversed as Lemarcus led Austin up the stairs and into the living room, where hip-hop music blasted as more attendees shared crack pipes, needles, and bottles of booze. The stench was overwhelming. Lemarcus covered his nose and mouth with a hand as he and Austin searched the entire first floor for Makayla and Shanice, but he didn't find them.

"They're probably upstairs," Lemarcus shouted over the music.

After searching the second floor, he opened the last door on the left at the end of a hallway, stepped into a bedroom, and Austin followed him in. He heard moans and whispers in a corner. The light from the hallway did not provide sufficient illumination. He hit the switch and a lamp across the room came on.

Hearing Austin close the door behind him, Lemarcus saw two twin beds in the room. On the bed nearest the window, across the room, Shanice lay atop a white man with his penis in her mouth. The man licked her asshole from behind. Both moaned in ecstasy with their eyes closed, and neither had noticed the lamp turn on.

On the bed nearest the door, right in front of Lemarcus, another white man had his face buried between Makayla's naked thighs, eating Lemarcus's eight-year-old daughter's pussy. Makayla's eyes were closed, and she was crying; tears leaked from the corners of each eye. Lemarcus wanted to torture the sick son of a bitch but knew he did not have time. Instead, drawing his gun, he grabbed a fistful of the man's hair, yanked him onto the floor, and shot him once through the back of his head, blowing his brains out the front of his skull.

To his left, interrupted by the gunfire, Shanice pulled the white man's penis out of her mouth. "What the fuck?"

Then he heard Makayla say, "Daddy!"

Aiming the gun at Shanice, Lemarcus looked down at his daughter.

No longer crying, she wore a smile on her face. Her clothes lay on the floor next to the bed.

"Get dressed, Makayla. We're leaving."

"Yay!" Makayla sprang from the bed and immediately put on her clothes.

Shanice said, "Oh, hell no. You're not taking my daughter anywhere."

Still pointing the gun at Shanice, Lemarcus told Austin, "Take Makayla out into the hallway. She don't need to see what I'm about to do."

"No, Daddy!" Makayla said. "I want to see you kill her! I wanna see her go to Hell, where she belongs."

Lemarcus shrugged. "Okay." Then he shot his wife and the other white man through their heads, killing them instantly.

CH. 10

With a broken heart, Justin sat on a bench at a bus station in South Carolina, trying to ignore the crowd moving past him, but too dejected to pay attention to the Dean Koontz paperback he held. He had purchased the book from a vendor on the strip at Myrtle Beach, and now it and his duffel bag were the only things he traveled with as he headed back to his parents' house in West Virginia. His girlfriend (ex-girlfriend, he reminded himself) had driven away with his suitcase still in her car when she left him.

Justin looked up at the order of arriving buses that flashed in yellow lights on an overhead sign. Soon thereafter, he boarded a bus for Charleston, West Virginia. He dropped into a seat halfway down.

Moments later, a beautiful blonde woman wearing a baseball cap, blue jeans, and a tank top stepped into the bus and made eye contact with him. She held a suitcase in one hand; a duffel bag hung from her opposite shoulder. As she walked forward, she ignored all the people on the seats that she passed. Reaching Justin's seat, she stopped and smiled down at him. "Mind if I sit with you?"

Justin held her gaze but did not return her smile. Then he shook his head and scooted over next to the window. "Be my guest."

"Thanks!" She put her suitcase in the luggage compartment above Justin's head, then sat next to him with the duffel bag on her lap. "I'm Britney. Why are you so sad?"

"I'm Justin. Nice to meet you. And I'm sad because my girlfriend just left me."

"I'm sorry to hear that."

"Yeah. She left me at the beach. It was our first road trip together and then, the first chance she gets, she runs off with somebody else. It makes no sense."

"Girls can be complete bitches sometimes," Britney said.

Justin nodded. "I'm crushed. Not even gonna lie. It's like a dream in which I'm running toward a place I'll never reach."

"Damn! Nice analogy. How old are you?"

"16."

Britney looked down at the book he was holding. "It's nice to see that teenagers still read."

He shrugged. "I'm the only teenager I know who does. How old are you?"

"24. And I love to read. I've been reading books since I was younger than you. And I love to write books, too."

Justin cocked his head. "You write books?"

"Yep. Sure do."

"What kinda books?"

She pointed at the book he was holding. "Stuff like that, mostly. Horror fiction. Although I much prefer the stuff Koontz wrote early in his career, back in the '80s and '90s. Everything after *Sole Survivor* was garbage."

Justin held the book up. "Is this one any good? I've only read the first few pages."

"That one? *Intensity*? That one's phenomenal. It's one of the last great novels he ever wrote. It was published in 1995. You're in for a treat."

He opened the book to the copyright page: **1995**. "Yep. You were right. You definitely know what you're talking about."

"Of course! If I don't know what I'm talking about, I keep my mouth shut. Anyway, there's a quote I love. It may have been Stephen King, but I can't remember. It goes something like this: 'For every one book you write, you need to read at least a hundred others.' And I'm a firm believer in that."

"I need to read some of your stuff sometime."

Britney shrugged. "We'll see. Where ya headed?"

"West Virginia."

"Me too! Which part are you from?"

"Charleston."

"I'm from Warlington. You know where that's at?"

"Yep. We passed by it on the way down here. It's about an hour south of where I live."

The bus jerked forward with a hiss of pneumatics, and then pulled away.

Justin flipped through the book to his current location. "I'm not looking forward to going home. I was hoping to be away from my parents for at least another week."

From her bag, Britney retrieved a book by an author he never heard of. "You don't get along with your parents?"

"No. Not at all. They don't like me very much, and the feeling is mutual."

"I live with my parents, too," Britney said. "But my parents are awesome. You'd love my parents."

"Must be nice."

"It is. My parents like to drink, take drugs, throw wild parties—all kinds of stuff."

"Damn! That sounds awesome!"

Britney laughed. "Never a dull moment, that's for damned sure." She opened her book, and then added, "You can come and stay with us for a while, if you want to."

"Seriously?"

"Sure! You can get off with me in Warlington, hang out with us for a while, then I can drive you back to Charleston whenever you're ready. I'll even give you a couple of my books to take home with you."

"Sweet!" Justin said. "I didn't wanna go home anyway."

She smiled. "You in a better mood now?"

"Hell, yeah! Absolutely."

She patted his leg twice. "Glad to hear that." She looked down at her book.

Justin glanced out the window, trying to ignore the rising of his penis beneath his jeans. Then he looked down at his book and tried to read.

CH. II

Lemarcus drove. Austin rode next to him on the passenger's side. Makayla was in the back.

Previously, Lemarcus had only seen the Winfield mansion—a series of structures that snaked up the mountain between jutting shelves of stone—from a distance. When they reached Holt Mountain Road, however, and began their ascent, he was stunned by the mansion's enormity and strange combination of organic and Gothic-revival architecture. Parts of the mansion stood out clearly from the rocks and trees, while others blended in and seemed to be a part of the mountain itself.

They ascended until they came to a stone wall that blocked all further progress. Within the stone wall were a pair of wrought-iron gates. Engraved in iron on a stone arch above the gates was the name **WESLEY WINFIELD**.

Austin—using the same Walmart burner phone with which he had called his father for permission to come home—called his father again and said, "We're here."

The gates swung open less than two seconds later.

After he drove through, Lemarcus saw the gates already closing in his rearview mirror. The design on the gates reminded him of a spider's web.

At the top of the mountain, Lemarcus was stunned when the mansion's main structure came into view. Sparks of moonlight glinted off numerous weathervanes and lightning rods mounted on the many slanted roofs. Behind him, Makayla said, "It looks like a castle!"

Lemarcus parked in the circular drive near the main entrance and killed the engine. "Are those your grandparents?" he asked, pointing to an older man and woman standing on the front porch.

"No," Austin said. "That's Atticus and Eleanor. Husband and wife. They've been working here longer than we've been alive."

"What do they do?"

"Just about everything. She's the lead housekeeper, and he's the chief of staff. Together, they oversee the maids, cooks, laundry workers, groundskeepers, security guards, you name it." Austin took a drink. Then he capped his bottle and opened the passenger door. "Come on. Let's go say hello."

They all three got out. Lemarcus took Makayla's hand and followed Austin up onto the front porch.

"Welcome home, Austin," Eleanor said as her husband nodded at Lemarcus and smiled. Then Eleanor looked down at Makayla, smiling. "And you must be Makayla. I'm Eleanor. It's so nice to meet you."

"It's nice to meet you, too," Makayla said.

Lemarcus knew that Austin had told his father their names on the burner phone, before he brought them here, and he figured that Wesley Winfield probably knew their dates of birth and social security numbers by now, also.

Eleanor told Lemarcus, "We prepared rooms for you and your daughter up on the fourth floor, next to Austin's room, on the west wing. My husband has your keys."

From a pocket of the sports coat he wore, Atticus produced two keys.

"Thank you very much," Lemarcus said. "We appreciate it."

"Each of your suites has a bathroom and a kitchenette," Eleanor explained. "We stocked your cabinets with food, and your refrigerators with beverages. If there's anything else you need, don't hesitate to let us know."

"They're gonna need clothes," Austin told her. "What they're wearing right now are the only clothes they have."

Eleanor nodded. "No problem. I'll send one of the girls shopping in the morning." From a breast pocket of the navy blouse she wore, Eleanor withdrew a notepad with a pen attached and opened it. "What size pants do you wear?" she asked Lemarcus.

"22/34. And I like my shirts in extra-large. And dark socks. I don't like white. And boxers, definitely. Not briefs."

She wrote it down. "Any favorite colors?"

Lemarcus shook his head. "Not really. Just dark colors, I guess. I'm not picky."

"And what about you, Makayla?" Eleanor asked. "What size clothes do you wear?"

"Size 8," Makayla said. "Like my age. I'm eight years old. And my favorite colors are pink, purple, and baby blue."

Eleanor wrote it down. "I'll have your clothes sent to your rooms tomorrow."

"Thanks again," Lemarcus said. "We appreciate it."

Atticus smiled. "Don't mention it. You're part of the family, now."

Austin told Lemarcus, "Come on. I'll show you to your rooms."

"Cool." Holding Makayla's hand, Lemarcus followed him inside.

Austin led them through a foyer with a white-and-gold marble floor, into a room that soared 40 feet to the ceiling. The floor featured limestone tiles, and the room was filled with antique furniture.

Lemarcus saw a grand piano to his right. To his left was a fireplace that undoubtedly emptied up into one of the many chimneys he had seen from outside. The room featured two spiral staircases. The one on the left, he assumed, ascended to the west wing, and the one on the right ascended to the east.

Austin led them up the staircase on the left, all the way up to the fourth floor, then down a wide hallway lined with doors. The doors on the left were closed, but all the doors on the right were open.

"We have ten suites on this floor," Austin said. "Five in the east wing, and five here in the west. The suites are on the left. All these rooms on the right are common rooms." He pointed to the first door on the left. "That's my sister's room, and my room's the last one down. So, the three in the middle are available, but Eleanor said she prepared the two rooms next to mine, so each of you can choose one of those."

"I'll take this one," Makayla said, pointing to the third door on the left.

Of the two keys Atticus gave him, the first one Lemarcus used opened the door. Then he gave the key to Makayla, and they all three stepped into the room.

"Wow, this is so nice!" Makayla said.

Lemarcus looked around. "It's like a suite at the Four Seasons."

Austin nodded. "Yep. The maids will clean your room every day if you want them to. They also supply toiletries as needed. You just have to let them know when you're running low. Oh, and breakfast, lunch, and dinner is served downstairs every day, but if you don't want to eat what's being served, you can always just eat whatever housekeeping stocks in your kitchenette."

A remote control lay on the coffee table. Makayla picked it up and turned on the TV. "I could live in this room forever. All I need now are some books."

"There's a library downstairs," Austin said.

Makayla asked her father, "Can we go down to the library?"

He nodded. "Of course. I need to find something to read, too."

"Come on," Austin said. "I'll show you where it's at."

They followed him to an elevator out in the hallway, then rode down from the fourth floor to the first. As they walked across the mansion, while Austin exchanged greetings with two maids, a security guard, and a maintenance man they passed, Lemarcus held his daughter's hand.

The library was massive, with a hardwood floor, Persian carpets, and armchairs arranged among mazes of shelves housing thousands of books. More books were shelved on a second level served by a catwalk that could be reached by an open staircase. Lemarcus looked up: moonlight glowed through a stained-glass dome in the ceiling.

"Come on," Austin said. "Dad's over there, by the fireplace."

As they approached him, Lemarcus recognized Wesley Winfield from the many times he had seen him in the news. In addition to being known as a ruthless crime lord, he was also known for his philanthropy, contributing generous donations to people and communities not only in the city of Warlington, but all throughout the state of West Virginia.

Wesley looked up from the book he was reading and smiled. He had to be almost 50 but looked much younger. His thick, dark hair was slicked back from his forehead. "Welcome home, son," he told Austin. Then he told Lemarcus, "And you must be the man who saved his life."

"Brought me back to life," Austin corrected. "Technically, I was dead."

Makayla looked up at Austin. "You were dead?"

"Yep. According to your father."

She looked up at Lemarcus. "Are you sure he was dead?"

"Yes, I'm sure he was dead. I checked for a pulse, and everything. He was gone, so I punched him in the chest and brought him back."

Makayla asked Austin, "Do you remember anything? About being dead?"

"Actually, I do." He took a drink from his bottle of whiskey. "But I don't have the words to describe it."

"How did you die?"

"He overdosed, Makayla," Lemarcus said. "That's why if I ever catch you taking drugs, I'll beat your fuckin' ass."

Makayla laughed. "You'll never catch me taking drugs. No way. I saw what drugs did to my mother."

Wesley closed his book, set it on the floor next to a bottle of bourbon, and rose from his armchair. "How old are you, Makayla?"

"I'm eight."

"And where's your mother right now?"

"My mother's in Hell, where she belongs."

Wesley looked at his son, smiling. "I like her." Then he told Lemarcus, "Your daughter's awfully smart for an eight-year-old."

Lemarcus shrugged. "She's an old soul. We both are."

Wesley nodded, still smiling. "Thanks for bringing my son back to life."

Lemarcus shrugged again. "Don't mention it. Like I said, I punched him in the chest, and he snapped right out of it. It was nothing."

"Nothing to you, maybe," Wesley said. "But everything to me. And for that, you'll always be welcome here. You can live here, work for me, and you and your daughter will have anything you need."

"Thanks," Lemarcus said. "We'll talk later. Right now, we're tired, and just came down here for some books. You know, something to read before we fall asleep."

"Of course."

Still holding Makayla's hand, Lemarcus led her into the maze of shelves.

CH. 12

On a Tuesday afternoon, while pushing her housekeeping cart along the Winfield mansion's second floor, Cassidy felt the baby kicking in her womb. It was at least seven months old, possibly eight, and she did not know its gender. The Winfields employed their own doctors at the mansion, but Wesley and his strange wife Nora told her they didn't want her to have an ultrasound, that they wanted the baby's gender to be a surprise.

Wesley was the baby's father. He and Nora paid her a large sum of money to be the surrogate mother, and now she just wanted the damned thing out of her. After delivering the baby, Cassidy intended to take the money and run. She was beginning to think the entire Winfield family was insane, and a part of her wished she had never started working here. It was a relief to know her employment was almost over.

While pushing her cart toward an elevator, she heard a familiar voice call her name, and she turned around.

Eleanor—the lead housekeeper (and whom Cassidy found equally as creepy as Wesley's wife)—was approaching from down the hallway.

Great, Cassidy thought. I'm seriously not in the mood for one of her lectures.

Smiling, Eleanor stopped three feet away. "Nora needs to see you in her office. I'll take your cart."

"Okay. Thank you." Cassidy took the elevator down to the first floor, and then went to Nora's office. The door was open, and she stepped inside. "You wanted to see me?"

Nora rose from the chair behind her desk. Wesley's wife, perhaps 20 years older than Cassidy, was still an attractive woman, but something in her eyes had always given Cassidy the creeps. Also, Cassidy had not been artificially inseminated, and the way Nora had watched her husband impregnate Cassidy had sort of freaked Cassidy out. While her husband had fucked Cassidy, Nora had watched from across the room with what appeared to be a mixture of detachment and curiosity. "Yes," Nora said. "One of our doctors would like to see you in the basement."

"In the basement?"

"Yes. He wants to do an ultrasound to monitor the baby's health. Follow me."

They stepped out of the office, then Nora led Cassidy to a freight elevator at the other end of the hallway, and they descended.

Illumination was dim. Cassidy followed Nora past the laundry room, the boiler room, the elevator-motor room, then down a hallway to a metal door she had never noticed before.

Using a key, Nora opened the door. "After you."

Cassidy stepped into a concrete room. Nora followed her in, then closed the door behind them and locked it.

Wesley stood in the room, along with a doctor that Cassidy had seen previously. Wesley wore street clothes. The doctor wore green medical scrubs. Both stood next to a mobile operating table in front of what looked like an incinerator—a cremation system perhaps, like those used in mortuaries. Surgical instruments lay arranged on a tray atop a cart next to the operating table, which was parked above a drain in the concrete floor. Cassidy looked around; she didn't see an ultrasound machine anywhere.

The doctor approached her, smiling, with his hands behind his back.

"He's gonna give you an injection," Wesley told her. "Just a little something to help you relax."

From behind his back, the doctor produced a hypodermic syringe, slipped the needle into a vein of Cassidy's left arm, and pressed the plunger.

She felt a burning pain in her arm. "What the hell was that?"

Nora approached her and grabbed a fistful of Cassidy's hair. "Rocuronium," she whispered. "A fast-acting paralytic."

"Paralytic? But I thought I was just having an ultrasound. What the—" Then her whole body went limp. She would have fallen, but Nora and the doctor prevented it. They dragged her to the operating table, slammed her down on top of it, and stripped her naked. Cassidy could still feel everything but was incapable of moving much more than her eyelids.

Wesley joined them at the table to stare down at her, smiling.

The doctor snapped on a pair of surgical gloves. "Spread her legs."

Nora grabbed one of her ankles. Wesley grabbed the other, and they spread her legs apart.

"The blocking agent I administered," the doctor told her, "only affects your movement. It will not cause the sedation of pain."

"In other words," Nora said, smiling, "you're gonna feel every goddamn bit of this."

The doctor sat down on a stool next to the medical cart. As he leaned in, Cassidy felt him use his fingers to separate her vaginal lips. Then she felt him shove a finger, then another, and then another of his free hand inside her, moving them in deep, and thrusting them in and out. "Just loosening you up," he explained.

Cassidy felt tears streaming down both sides of her face.

Horrified, she watched the doctor retrieve a speculum from the medical cart and lubricate it with Vaseline. Paralyzed, she still saw Wesley and Nora watching the doctor's every move. He inserted the speculum, shoved it deep inside, then spread her vaginal walls so that all three of them could see inside her. Pain exploded through her cervix, and she felt fluids gushing down her ass.

"Blood," Nora said. "So much beautiful blood."

As the doctor reached a hand inside her, Cassidy felt the baby kick, as if trying to escape him. Yanking his hand back out, he grabbed a surgical instrument with a sharp hook on its end.

"I want the placenta," Nora said. "I want to feel it and taste it in my mouth. All those vitamins and nutrients in the fetal fluids. So delicious."

"I'm gonna raise the table," Wesley said. "So she can see better." He quickly raised the table to a half-seated position, then rejoined his wife and doctor at Cassidy's feet.

The doctor shoved the hooked end of the instrument into her vagina. Pain erupted in her uterus as he began scraping its walls. Blood started pouring, and he removed the hooked instrument. He caught the placenta when it slipped out, handed it to Nora, and she immediately began eating it.

The baby came out next, and he severed the umbilical cord with a scalpel. Cassidy saw that her mangled infant was still alive. She wanted to scream when she saw her baby cradled in the doctor's hands, but she was unable.

Wesley pulled out his penis and began stroking it. "Give me the goddamn baby."

The doctor placed the baby—small and premature—in Wesley's free hand. While he masturbated with the other, Wesley licked amniotic fluids and remnants of the placenta from the baby's head. "Oh God," he said. "Oh God, I'm gonna come."

He leaned his head back and shuddered as ropes of semen shot out of his penis and onto the baby's newly opened eyes.

It screamed and Wesley tore out its throat with his teeth before eating its face.

Finished with the placenta, Nora knelt at the end of the table and buried her face in Cassidy's vagina. She licked and slurped for several seconds, then raised her head, smiling. Her face was covered with gore and chunks of flesh. "Are we gonna kill this bitch, or is she a keeper?"

"We'll keep her," Wesley said. "She'll provide us with placentas and fresh babies for years to come." He pitched the infant's corpse into the incinerator and pulled his pants up. Then he told the doctor, "Let's take her down to the subbasement with the others."

Wesley opened the door, and Cassidy watched him hold it for the doctor as he pushed her operating table out into the hallway. She could hear Nora pushing the medical cart behind them as she followed them out of the room. Then they all rode an elevator Cassidy had never seen before down another floor to the subbasement.

"Why are you doing this to me?" Cassidy whispered after they wheeled her into a filthy room that stank of human waste and rancid flesh. Every nerve in her body seemed to be screaming in agony.

"The paralytic's wearing off," the doctor said. "Want me to amputate her limbs?"

Wesley nodded. "Yes. But first, give her a tracheotomy. We'll stick a breathing tube in her neck. That way, she won't be able to scream, but she can still whisper, if we cover the tube."

The doctor shot her up with more rocuronium, and soon she was unable to move again. Then he performed the tracheotomy with a scalpel, cutting a hole in her neck, creating a new airway, and inserting a breathing tube in her throat. By the time he finished, the paralytic's effects were diminishing, and she was able to move her head from side to side.

"Want me to start her on an IV drip?" the doctor asked Wesley. "An antibiotic? Before we begin the amputations?"

Wesley picked up a blowtorch from the medical cart and turned it on. Cassidy thought its blue flame looked like a bolt of lightning.

"No," Wesley said. "You cut. We'll cauterize. She'll be fine."

The doctor selected a bone saw from the medical cart and raised it. Horrified, Cassidy looked away—and saw four other pregnant women lying on the floor, limbless, with cauterized stumps and breathing tubes sticking out of their necks.

Then, pain that eclipsed everything else began.

CH. 13

An hour south of where he lived in Charleston, Justin got off the bus with Britney in Warlington, West Virginia.

An old man driving a Bentley picked them up at the bus station.

Expensive car, Justin thought, as he climbed into the back.

Britney put her luggage in the trunk, then got into the passenger's side. "Hello, Atticus. Thanks for picking us up! This is my new friend, Justin. He's gonna be staying with us for a while."

Atticus looked at Justin in the rearview mirror. "It's nice to meet you."

"It's nice to meet you too," Justin said.

Fifteen minutes later, at the top of a mountain, Atticus parked in front of the biggest house Justin had ever seen.

They got out and went inside. Justin followed Atticus and Britney through a foyer into a room that soared 40 feet to the ceiling, where an old woman greeted them, smiling. When Atticus put an arm around her waist, Justin assumed they were a couple.

"Welcome home, Britney," the woman said.

"Thank you, Eleanor! It's great to be back. And this is my new friend, Justin. He's gonna be staying with us for a while."

"It's nice to meet you, Justin."

"It's nice to meet you, too."

Eleanor told Britney, "Your brother brought two people home a few days ago."

"Is that right?"

"Yes. A young man and his daughter. We put them on the fourth floor, between yours and your brother's suites, but the one right next to yours is still available."

"Perfect!" Britney said. Then she turned to Justin. "Come on. I'll show you to your room."

He followed her to a staircase on the left, and they ascended to the fourth floor, where a young girl with brown skin dribbled a basketball in the hallway. Justin thought she couldn't have been older than seven or eight. He also thought she handled the basketball well for her age. She stopped dribbling when she saw them, and just stared.

"Hello! I'm Britney, and this is Justin. What's your name?"

"Makayla."

"It's great to meet you, Makayla! Eleanor told us that my brother brought a young man and his daughter to stay with us, so she must have been talking about you. Where's your father?"

"Passed out."

"Passed out? Is he okay?"

Makayla tossed the basketball from her right hand to her left. "He's fine. My dad's an alcoholic. Other than that, he's an amazing guy."

Britney laughed. "Hell, yeah! I'm an alcoholic, too! Sounds like your dad and I will get along just fine." Then she asked Justin, "What about you? You like to drink?"

Justin shook his head. "I hate the taste of beer."

Makayla told Britney, "I need something to read. I couldn't find any good books down in the library. Austin said you have all the good books in your room."

Britney cocked her head. "How old are you, Makayla?"

"I'm eight."

"Well, my brother also should have told you that most of the books in my room are horror fiction. Adult horror fiction. Probably not suitable for an eight-year-old."

"That's all I read," Makayla said. "Stephen King and Dean Koontz are my favorites."

"Seriously?"

"Yes. My dad's an English teacher. He says I'm precocious. I've been reading adult fiction since I was six."

Justin had never heard the word "precocious," but if it meant "smart for your age," then yes, he believed Makayla was precocious.

Setting her suitcase on the floor, Britney opened the door to her suite with a key. "Fine. Come on in. I'm sure you'll find something to your liking."

Makayla followed her in.

Closing the door behind him, Justin entered the suite, which was set up like an efficiency apartment. Overflowing bookshelves lined the walls, and stacks of more books filled most of the suite's available space.

"This place is awesome!" Makayla said. She immediately began wandering around.

There was not a solid separation between the bedroom space and the living area. After Britney put her suitcase and duffel bag on the bed, Justin set his duffel bag on the floor, next to the coffee table.

Makayla, still holding the basketball, picked out a Stephen King paperback with a cat on its cover. "*Pet Sematary*," she said. "Dad says this one is good."

Britney nodded. "It's one of my favorites." From her bag, she retrieved a bottle of clear liquor and cracked it open.

Justin told Britney, "I wanna read one of the books you wrote."

Makayla asked Britney, "You write books?"

"Yep. Sure do."

"My dad writes books, too," Makayla said. "But he told me I can't read his books until I'm older."

Britney took a drink. "That makes sense to me."

Makayla shrugged. "I guess. Anyway, thanks for the book. I'll bring it back when I'm finished."

"You're welcome," Britney said.

Makayla left.

Britney set the bottle on her nightstand, then shoved her duffel bag and suitcase under the bed and stretched out on the mattress. She grabbed a remote and turned on the TV. "Come over here." She patted the mattress. "I don't bite."

Justin joined her on the bed, with his back against the headboard, facing the TV, trying to ignore his rising penis.

"What do you like to watch?" Britney asked him.

"Nothing, really. I don't watch TV."

"Me neither. It's mainly just background noise." She put down the remote, grabbed her bottle, and took a drink.

"What are you drinking, anyway?"

"Vodka. Want some?"

"Sure."

She handed him the bottle.

He took a drink, grimaced, and started coughing. "Oh, wow. That is really strong."

Britney laughed. "Hell yeah, dude! 100 proof. It's a lot better than beer though. Am I right?"

"Yes. Definitely." Justin took another drink and gave the bottle back. "So, what do you people do, anyway? Apparently, you have more money than God."

"Can't tell you that." She set the bottle on her nightstand. "If I told you that, I'd have to kill you." Then she put a hand on his thigh. "And I don't wanna kill you. I'd rather fuck your brains out."

"Is that right?"

"Yes. Are you a virgin?"

"Nope. Not even close."

"Have you ever fucked an older woman before?"

Justin cocked his head. "You're only 24. But yes, I fucked a student teacher two years ago, in eighth grade. I was 14. She was 22."

"Sweet! Now I won't feel like such a pedophile."

He grabbed her hand and pressed it against his erection. "Wanna get naked?"

She smiled. "I thought you'd never ask."

CH. 14

Sleep had eluded Peg for most of the night, and she woke to the glaring light of dawn. Before the fire, insomnia had been a stranger, but now, she rarely slept. These days, what minimal sleep she attained was filled with nightmares of her family, ghosts that existed only in her memories and her dreams.

She retrieved a bottle of rum from underneath her bed, then swallowed long and hard before she rose to face the day.

By noon, Peg was drunk. By 6 PM, she was in no condition to drive to her 7 o'clock loss-of-child support group meeting in the basement of a church down the street. At 6:30, she poured out half a bottle of soda, filled it with rum, and took off walking.

Austin parked in front of the church and went inside.

Fifteen minutes later, the group sat around a large room in the basement, drinking coffee and telling each other stories. Some in attendance wept, but not Austin. He didn't drink coffee either. Nor did he speak. He mainly just listened to the other people and tried not to stare at the woman he had seen here the previous Tuesday, on loss-of-spouse night. First Tuesdays of the month were for the loss-of-spouse meetings; second Tuesdays were for the loss-of-a-child. Apparently, like him, she had lost both.

Outside, after the meeting's conclusion, she stopped him on his way to his car. "Excuse me," she said. "I know who you are."

"Is that so?"

"Yes. You're Austin Winfield. You lost your wife and daughter in a car crash two years ago."

"Then I'm afraid you have me at a disadvantage."

"I'm Peg. I lost my son, my daughter, and my husband six months ago. They were murdered."

"I'm sorry to hear that," Austin said. "Would you like to talk about it?"

She shrugged. "I don't know. Maybe. I mean, I don't even know what I'm doing anymore."

He looked down at the bottle of soda she was holding. "You smell like you've been drinking."

"Yeah. I stay drunk all the time, these days. That's why I walked here. Can you give me a ride home? I just live right down the street."

"Sure."

They got in Austin's car.

"I figured you'd drive a more expensive vehicle," Peg said from the passenger's side.

Austin started the engine. "This car isn't exactly cheap."

"Yeah, I know that, but you're a Winfield, for God's sake. I figured you'd be driving a Rolls-Royce or a Lamborghini."

He shook his head. "I'm not as flashy as the rest of my family. Plus, I prefer keeping a low profile." Austin put the car on the road, and they arrived at Peg's house down the street moments later.

"Wanna come in?" she asked him in the driveway. "I have plenty of rum."

"Sure." He killed the engine.

They got out and went inside.

Austin looked around. "Nice place."

Then a small, long-haired, black-and-white dog with floppy ears entered the living room and looked up at him, tail wagging. The dog wore a pink collar. "She's beautiful," Austin said. "What's her name?"

"Zoey. She's a Yorkie-poo, a cross between a Yorkshire terrier and a miniature poodle. Do you like rum?"

"Yes, I do like rum, actually." He followed her into the kitchen, where Peg withdrew a bottle of rum from a cabinet.

"There's some soda in the fridge," she said. "I can make you a drink if you want, but I normally just drink mine straight."

"Nah, that's okay. Straight's cool with me."

Peg filled two tumblers with rum, handed one to Austin, then looked down at Zoey, who was looking up at Austin with her tail wagging. "She likes you."

He bent down and scratched Zoey's head. "I like her, too." In the living room, he stopped in front of a portrait of Peg with a black man and two biracial children—a young boy and an even younger girl. He sipped his rum. "Beautiful family. I'm sorry for your loss."

"Our last photo together. It was taken about a month before they died."

Peg sat down on the sofa, and Austin joined her on its opposite end. Two seconds later, Zoey jumped up to sit on the cushion between them.

"My husband," Peg said, staring at the portrait, "was the first African American judge in the history of Wickham County."

"Wickham County?"

"Yes. Up north. Close to Morgantown."

"I know where it is." Austin sipped his rum. "Wickham County is not a friendly place."

"Tell me about it. It remains a hotbed of white supremacy even in this day and age. But Malcolm was even fair to the racists who despised him. I used to tell him he was honorable to a fault."

Austin shot her a look. "How old are you?"

"31."

"Ah, okay. I'm 27. I thought you were closer to my age."

"No. And Malcolm was ten years older than me. I met him at the Wickham County Courthouse. I took a job there as a stenographer, after I graduated from WVU. I was 22 and he had just been appointed judge at 32."

"That's awfully young to become a judge."

"Yes, but not unheard of. The youngest person ever appointed judge was 24."

Zoey put her head on Austin's lap, and he rubbed it. "You said your family was murdered six months ago."

Peg sipped her drink. "Yes, in Wickham County. This house was my mother's. She died six months ago, too. Natural causes. I moved back here after my family was murdered."

"Do you know who killed them?"

"Yes, I do. The Ku Klux Klan killed my family."

"The KKK? Seriously?"

"Yes. Would you like to hear the story?"

"Sure."

"Okay." Peg took a drink. "I had never trusted the citizens of Wickham County. You already know how the people are in that place—racist, homophobic, et cetera. So of course they looked down on me for marrying a black man. I saw the looks they gave my children in the grocery store and heard their snide remarks behind our backs. And my mother was the same way—opposed to interracial relationships. She disapproved of my marriage to Malcolm and looked down on our children as some sort of crossbred mutants. She never wanted anything to do with her grandchildren."

"I'm sorry to hear that," Austin said.

Peg took a drink. "When the doctor called and told me that Mom was dying, I didn't even want to go say goodbye. It was Malcolm who convinced me to go see her, even though she despised him and our kids. 'She's your mother,' he said. 'You may never get a chance to make amends.' And so, I came here, alone, to say goodbye to my mother, and then she died. I stuck around for the funeral. By convincing me to come here, Malcolm saved my life." She paused to take a drink, and then continued. "When I got home, our house was in ruins. There was nothing left but its smoldering structural remains. I was told later that all three of them were found in my daughter's bedroom. Beth Ann was four. Michael, seven, was found on top of her, as protective of his little sister in death as he had been in life. Malcolm was found on top of them both as if hoping he could save them."

Austin sipped his drink. "So, it was arson?"

"Yes. Shortly before the blaze, a jury convicted a white man of first-degree murder. The victim had been a black man. Malcolm sentenced the white man to life without parole. And the KKK struck a match. Simple as that."

Austin put a hand on her shoulder. "I wish I could ease your pain."

"Yeah, me too." Peg sipped her drink. "I often imagine how it must have happened. In the waning darkness before the dawn of that godforsaken day, some members of the local chapter doused the entire house with gasoline, then sealed all exits with flames. Malcolm, Michael, and Beth Ann never had a chance. I can close my eyes and hear the smoke alarms blasting the stillness of the morning, and see tongues of flame licking every window, every door. I can feel the increasing heat as the oxygen diminishes. I see the little girl who, in the end, ran back to her room to be with her dolls, and the brother and the father who followed her there."

Austin finished his drink. "Maybe you'll see them again, in the next life. And maybe I'll see my family again, too."

"It's possible." Peg reached down and rubbed Zoey's head. "In the meantime, I'll have little Fuzz Face here to keep me company." She finished her drink and rose from the sofa. "Ready for a refill?"

"Sure."

She brought the bottle in from the kitchen, refilled their glasses, and sat back down.

"I used to not believe in an afterlife," Peg said. "My mother was very religious, and I rejected her Christian faith. It's funny how losing everyone you love can make you change your belief system."

He nodded. "Absolutely."

Peg took a drink. "I used to place all my faith in science, in the study of our universe through experiment and observation, but science doesn't know all the answers. It doesn't know where the laws of nature came from. It doesn't know why the universe began, or if it even had a beginning. But if it did begin with a big bang fourteen-billion years ago, I'm inclined to believe that something created the big bang. Was it God? I don't know. But if God said, 'Let there be light,' I imagine there would be a big bang. Does that make sense?"

Austin shrugged. "I suppose."

"And if the universe had no beginning," Peg went on, "if it really is eternal, which it might be, then maybe its creator is eternal, and the universe has always been its home. Or maybe I'm just drunk and need to get laid."

Austin cracked a smile. "Maybe so."

"What about you?" she asked him. "Have you dated anyone since your wife died?"

"Nope. Been single for two years."

Peg's eyes widened. "You haven't had sex in two years?"

Austin shot her a look. "I said I've been single for two years, not celibate."

Peg finished her drink. Then she set her glass down and stood up. "I've been celibate for six months. You wanna fix that for me?"

Austin stood up, too. "I can do that."

She took his hand and led him into her bedroom.

CH. 15

Lemarcus woke up and checked his phone: **6:16 PM**. There was a bottle of whiskey on his nightstand, and he took a drink. Then he got up, took a shower, and got dressed, not surprised to find his daughter reading in the living room. He had been leaving his door unlocked, allowing her to come and go as she pleased, and Makayla spent as much time in his suite as her own. She was reading a book that had traumatized Lemarcus as a child, *Pet Sematary* by Stephen King, although Lemarcus had been twelve years old when he read it, not eight.

She gazed up at him with a look of trepidation. "This book is crazy. It's giving me the creeps."

He joined her on the sofa. "Did you find that down in the library?"

"No. Britney let me borrow it."

"Britney? Austin's sister?"

Makayla nodded. "She just got back in town. Her room's two doors down from mine. She has all kinds of scary books. I think you'll like her. She told me she's an alcoholic like you."

Lemarcus took a drink, then set his bottle on the coffee table. "Austin told me his sister's insane."

"The whole world's insane. What else is new? She brought a friend home, too. A boy."

"A boy?"

"Yes. His name is Justin. He's younger than her. 16, I think."

"White or black?"

"White. He's staying in the room next to mine."

Lemarcus shot her a look. "Is he cool?"

"Yes. He likes to read, too."

"Well, you let me know right away if he says anything inappropriate, or makes you feel uncomfortable in any way. Okay?"

"I will, Dad. But don't worry. Justin actually seems like an okay guy."

Lemarcus nodded, pleased that his daughter still had faith in the decency of others after the horrors her own mother subjected her to.

Makayla looked back down at *Pet Sematary*. "Two words from this book will haunt me forever."

He already knew what she was talking about but decided to play along. "And what two words are those?"

"'Gage's shoe,'" Makayla said.

Lemarcus nodded. "Brutal. Gage died when he was two, chasing a kite. Chased it right out into the road and got killed by a tanker truck."

"How come you never flew a kite with me when I was that age?"

"Well, gee, Makayla. Let's see. Maybe because I read the book—*almost a decade before I even became a parent*—and it fucked me up so bad that I never wanted to see another kite in my goddamn life. Sorry about my language."

"That's okay. My favorite rappers cuss all the time."

"Yeah, I know. But I still feel guilty, like I shouldn't do it. I should set a better example."

"That's okay, Dad. It's no big deal. They're only words."

From the coffee table, Lemarcus picked up the book he was reading: *We Have Always Lived in the Castle* by Shirley Jackson.

Makayla said, "You know how I only listen to the old rappers? All older music?"

"Of course."

"Well, apparently, I'm not the only one. I was reading an article the other day and the latest numbers say old songs make up 70% of the U.S. music market right now."

"I saw that," Lemarcus said. "And the 200 most popular new songs account for less than 5% of total streams. It's fucking crazy. Sorry about my language."

"It's okay, Dad. I love you."

"I love you, too."

They proceeded to read.

CH. 16

For the first time in his 16 years on Earth, Justin was in love. There was nothing about Britney he did not adore: the way she looked at him, as if gazing into his soul; the way their naked bodies perfectly fit together on her bed; the heat of her kisses, the taste of her skin, and the feel of her sweat as it dripped onto his flesh while she rode him to states of ecstasy.

He hoped their eight-year age difference didn't bother Britney, for it certainly did not bother him. She was the first thing he thought of when waking up, and the last thing on his mind before he slept.

An additional benefit was the fact that Britney was a great writer. He had finished reading one of her novels earlier that day and was looking forward to reading many more. He hoped to spend the rest of his life with Britney.

"I don't ever wanna go home," Justin told her, reading on the sofa in her suite.

Britney, writing beside him, didn't look up from her laptop. "Careful what you wish for, lover boy."

He laughed. "I'm serious. Fuck going back to Charleston. I just wanna stay with you forever."

She smiled. "That can be arranged." Moments later, she closed her laptop and rose from the sofa. "I have some errands to run tonight. I won't be back until late. Would you like another one of my books to read while I'm away?"

He considered asking if he could go with her but decided against it. "Sure."

She crossed the room, grabbed a book, and brought it to him. "See you later."

I love you, Justin thought.

He watched her walk away.

CH. 17

Warlington Police Chief Bruno Voss, still in uniform, entered the liquor store ten minutes before it closed. The cashier, a teenage boy whose name he couldn't remember, was mopping the floor and there was no one else inside.

The boy parked his mop bucket and headed toward the cash register. "Working late tonight, Chief?"

Voss nodded. In addition to all the administrative duties that came with being the chief, he also enjoyed performing the same duties (patrols, investigations, making arrests) as the regular officers. "No rest for the wicked." He grabbed a bottle of whiskey and set it on the counter. "I'll sleep when I'm dead."

The boy scanned the bottle and told him its price.

"Put it on my tab," Voss said. Then he gave the boy a hundred-dollar bill. "And this is for you. For being so nice."

"Thanks, Chief!"

Voss grabbed the bottle. "Don't mention it."

He left.

Fifteen minutes later, with a few shots in his system, Voss was in a better mood, and wanted to celebrate. He drove his squad car downtown and found a prostitute leaning against a lamppost. She wore a black miniskirt and a yellow tank top that accentuated her breasts. He couldn't remember her name, but he had fucked her a few times before. Tonight would be the last time, he decided. He stopped the car, told her to get in, and she did.

While he drove, Voss turned on the radio, scanned through the stations, and then switched it off.

"Where are we going?" the prostitute asked.

They were on a narrow, paved road headed out of town.

"Fitzpatrick Lake," Voss said. "No one will bother us there."

"Mind if I smoke ice in your car?"

"Go right ahead."

He heard her unzip her purse and glanced over. In the moonlight through the windshield, he watched her retrieve a lightbulb converted to a meth pipe. He put his eyes back on the road and heard her roll the spark wheel of a cigarette lighter down. A second later, he smelled the burning-plastic stench of crystal meth.

They arrived at Fitzpatrick Lake soon thereafter, and he killed the engine.

"You wanna hit this?" she asked him.

"Sure."

She packed the pipe and handed it to him, along with her cigarette lighter.

Voss quickly smoked the meth, and the ice hit him immediately. His whiskey buzz was gone, replaced by a soaring euphoria. He had always enjoyed smoking meth: the high was like a cocaine buzz, but a whole lot more intense.

She put the pipe back in her purse and withdrew a condom. "You wanna fuck up here, or in the back?"

"On the hood," Voss said.

They got out.

A full moon lit the mist rising off the lake.

"Someone left their boat," the prostitute said, nodding toward a rowboat with two oars lying on the shore.

"It's mine," Voss said, pulling his pants down. "Don't worry about it." He raised her skirt and fucked her on the hood, with his pants around his ankles. The sex lasted two minutes, tops.

Then he strangled her and fucked her corpse.

Afterward, he retrieved two cinderblocks and two chains from the trunk of his squad car, chained a block to each of her ankles, rowed her out to the middle of the lake, and dropped her in.

Later, while driving back to Warlington, he saw a Ferrari parked on the side of the road with its hazard lights flashing. Turning his blue-and-red roof lights on, Voss parked his squad car behind the Ferrari and got out.

Approaching the car, he looked around, making sure he didn't see any witnesses.

He did not. In fact, he hadn't passed a single vehicle on this lonely road. He walked to the driver's-side door, pleased to see that the window was already down. A young woman looked up at him, smiling, which caught him off guard at first. "Britney Winfield? Jesus Christ, girl, I about didn't recognize you in that pink wig. And what are you doing in a blue Ferrari? I thought your Ferrari was red."

"I have a few Ferraris," Britney said.

He laughed. "Yeah, I guess you do. Anyway, is everything okay with this one?"

"Of course. Why do you ask?"

"Because you're parked on the side of the road with your hazard lights on. I thought maybe your car broke down."

"Nope. Nothing wrong with this car, that's for damned sure."

"Then why are you parked with your hazards flashing?"

"I'm a spider," she said. "Trying to catch some flies. Sort of like you with a radar gun."

"Is that right?"

"Yep, except I'm not trying to catch people driving over the speed limit. I'm trying to catch me a good Samaritan."

"Good Samaritan?"

"Yes. I figure if I sit here pretending to be having car troubles, some idiotic good Samaritan will come along, and then I can torture him and kill him."

"I just killed a hooker and stole her meth," Voss said. "You wanna smoke some?"

"Hell yeah! Hop on in."

Voss got in her car, and they passed the lightbulb converted to a meth pipe back and forth a couple times.

"Goddamn!" Britney said. "That's some good fucking meth."

Voss lit a cigarette. "Listen, I need you to stop leaving so many corpses all over the city."

"What the fuck are you talking about? No one tells me what to do. I'll do what the hell I want."

"I don't have a problem with that, Britney. But people are freaking out. You're leaving corpses all over with their organs missing. We're finding bodies with no brains, no livers, no spleens. The eyeballs have been removed. The teeth are missing. The jawbones have been sawed out. The genitalia's been cut away. People are calling you The Harvester."

"The Harvester?"

"Yes. They think there's a serial killer in town harvesting organs. Everyone thinks the killer's a man, but of course I know it's you, so don't even try to deny it. And I'm not mad, or anything. I just need you to stop being so cocky about it, to stop leaving the corpses out in the open where everyone can see them. I'm the one who has to deal with all this bullshit."

Britney lit a cigarette. "Listen, pig, my family pays you a lot of money to deal with this bullshit, so I don't think you have any right to complain."

"I'm not complaining. I'm just asking you to tone it down a little bit. I mean, Jesus Christ, Britney, I know your family's involved in organ trafficking, but I also know that your dad has his own team of harvesters living inside the mansion, and that they dispose of the corpses properly down in the basement, in the incinerator."

"What they do," Britney said, "and what *I* do are completely different. They do it for business. I do it for pleasure. So, unless you wanna become one of my victims, I suggest you stop harassing me with this bullshit."

Voss put his hands up. "Fine. The last thing I wanna do is end up on your bad side." He started to get out.

"Wait," Britney said. "Can I have the rest of that meth?"

"Sure." He gave her the ice and the lightbulb meth pipe. "Have a nice night."

Britney smoked more meth behind the steering wheel, watching the taillights of Bruno Voss's squad car disappear. Then another car pulled over onto the road's shoulder behind her Ferrari. Grabbing her duffel bag, she turned the hazard lights off and got out, not giving the driver of the other car—an older-model sedan—a chance to get out and approach her vehicle.

As Britney approached the sedan, she saw the silhouette of a man behind the steering wheel. The passenger's-side window came down, and he leaned over. "That's an awfully nice car you're driving. Did it break down on ya?" He was a white man with brown hair. Clean-shaven. Mid-twenties.

"I ran outta gas." It was the first lie that popped into her head. "I wasn't paying attention."

He nodded. "I got a gas can in the trunk, but it's damned near empty. I can give you a ride to a service station, though, and we can fill it up."

"Thanks! That would be great." She opened the passenger door and got in.

He put the car back on the road. "I'm Cooper, by the way. What's your name?"

She turned in her seat to face him, with her back against the door. "I'm Britney." Then she pulled a pistol from her duffel bag and aimed it at his face. "And this is a carjacking, by the way."

He turned his head, saw the gun, and his eyes widened in the moonlight. "Holy shit! Is that a .40 caliber?"

"Yes. Do exactly as I say, and I might let you live."

He put his eyes back on the road. "No problem. I got a wife and a daughter at home, so your wish is my command. Just tell me what to do, and I will do it."

"Good." She lowered the gun, but kept it aimed at his midsection. "Right now, I just need you to drive, until I figure out what to do."

Cooper drove.

"I've been smoking meth," Britney said, "and I'm in the mood to go on a killing spree."

"A killing spree?"

"Yes, but I have so many people on my hit list, I don't even know where to begin."

"There's a few people I'd like to see killed," Cooper said. "And every one of them hang out at the Hideaway Lounge."

"Hideaway Lounge? That shitkicker dive on Sullivan Road? Near the county line?"

"That's the one. I've had problems with the boys who've run that place for most of my goddamn life. The owner, David Black. The brothers who tend bar, Ralph and Dennis Adkins. The two dipshits who run security, Mike Elmore and Philip Cole. I hate every one of those sons of bitches. Do you know any of those boys?"

"Actually," she said, "I know them all."

He shot her a look. "Seriously?"

Britney laughed. "Honey, I know everyone in Warlington. I'm surprised I don't know you."

Cooper shrugged, focused on the road. "Yeah, well, I don't get out much, and those cocksuckers are the biggest reason why."

"You'll have to tell me about it," Britney said. "But first, find somewhere to pull over. I feel like getting high."

He found a lay-by past a signpost and pulled over, leaving the engine running. "Is this okay?"

"Perfect." Still pointing the gun at his midsection, she reached into the duffel bag with her other hand and withdrew the lightbulb converted to a meth pipe. "Here," she said, proffering the meth pipe. "Take this."

He did.

Then she put some meth inside the pipe and handed him a lighter. "Here's the deal," she said. "You're gonna hold the pipe and light it for me while I smoke, and if you make one wrong move"—she pressed the muzzle of the gun to his chest—"I'll blow your fuckin' heart out your back. Do you understand me?"

"Yes. But what about the cops? Do you think it's safe here?"

"Safe?"

"Yes. If a cop drives by, and sees us parked here, they might stop, and they'll be able to smell the meth."

Britney laughed. "Do you know who I am?"

"No, I don't."

"I'm someone who doesn't give a fuck about the cops. Trust me, the Warlington Police are on my payroll. Now shut the fuck up and light the pipe."

He did, and Britney smoked it.

Then she put more meth in and told him, "Your turn."

"You want me to smoke some?"

"Yes, and then I want you to tell me why you hate those boys from Hideaway Lounge. Have you ever smoked meth before?"

"Yes, a few times."

"Good. Then you know what to do."

Cooper smoked the meth at gunpoint.

Then Britney returned the pipe to her duffel bag. "Okay. Now you can tell me the story."

"You mind if I light a cigarette?"

She leaned back against the passenger door, facing him, with her gun pointed at his midsection. "Go right ahead."

He took a cigarette from his pack and lit it, then cracked open the driver's-side window. "Does the name Robert Morgan mean anything to you?"

Britney shook her head. "Nope, can't say it does."

"He's dead. Been dead for years. But long ago, when I was a kid, he owned a landscaping company in the neighborhood I grew up in."

"Here in Warlington?"

"Yep. Circleview Drive. Know where that's at?"

"Yes, off Harper Road. Near Mount Tabor Drive."

Cooper nodded. "Robert Morgan's landscaping company was basically just an old beat-up truck with lawnmowers and weed-eaters in the back. He lived in a singlewide trailer at the end of a private driveway. He used to hire neighborhood boys to work for him and pay them under the table. I was one of those boys. And so were David Black, Philip Cole, Mike Elmore, and Ralph and Dennis Adkins. We'd ride our bikes to his trailer in the mornings, and he'd drive us all over town to cut grass all day, and then we'd go back to his trailer in the evenings, where he'd give us alcohol, cigarettes, marijuana, pills, you name it. And it was fun! Know what I mean? We were kids, and it was exciting. And of course, there were rumors going around that he was a child molester, and I saw him take the other boys into his bedroom all the time, but they went willingly and seemed to be having a good time. And he never messed with me, so I just ignored that aspect of the situation."

"Let me guess," Britney said. "One day, he started molesting you."

"Yes, and it happened more than once. I quit working for him, but my parents could tell that something was wrong with me, and when I told them what happened, they went to the police."

"And the other boys got mad at you, didn't they?"

"Yes. That's an understatement, actually. I was the one who testified against him at his trial. The other boys lied and swore he never touched them, but the jury didn't buy it. Robert Morgan got convicted and ended up getting beaten to death in prison."

"And the other boys made your life a living Hell ever since."

"Yep. Pretty much." Cooper finished his cigarette and flipped it out the window.

"I'll tell you what," Britney said. "Since I wanna go on a killing spree, and you wanna see them dead, you're gonna drive me to the Hideaway Lounge, and I'm gonna kill all five of those bastards for you."

"Seriously?"

"Yes. If they're all there, I'll kill them all. But first, we're gonna smoke some more meth."

She pulled the pipe out of her duffel bag. "Same as before. One wrong move and I'll kill your ass instead."

"No problem."

At gunpoint, Cooper kept the pipe lit while they took turns hitting it. Then Britney returned the pipe to her duffel bag.

"Goddamn," Cooper said. "That's some killer fucking meth."

"Yes. Now take me to the Hideaway Lounge."

Cooper drove them back to town, and they headed south toward the county line. Fifteen minutes later, they arrived at the Hideaway Lounge.

By the glow of security lights on utility poles in the parking lot, they saw a group of maybe 20 people watching something happening in the middle of the group, about ten feet from the front door of the club.

"Someone's fighting," Cooper said. "Fights break out at this place all the time."

"Put the car in park," Britney said.

Cooper did, leaving the engine running.

In the twin beams of the headlights, David Black, Mike Elmore, Philip Cole, and Ralph and Dennis Adkins were part of the mob about 30 feet straight ahead.

"The gang's all here."

Britney told Cooper, "Get in over here on my side. We're switching places. If you try to run, I swear I'll shoot you first."

He got out, and Britney climbed into the driver's seat.

Cooper got back in on the passenger's side and closed the door. "This is the only car I have."

"I'll buy you a new one," Britney said. "Or you can have my Ferrari. It doesn't matter." She put the car in drive and floored the accelerator. The car shot forward and the crowd parted, leaving David Black exposed. The front end caught him at waist-level and pushed him back, the upper part of his body draped over the hood, his surprised eyes staring into Britney's from three feet away.

Then the car smashed into the brick wall of the building, chopping his body in half. The car came to a stop, and Britney watched the life go out of his eyes.

She backed the car up and his torso slid off the hood onto the parking lot, leaving a splash of gore that steamed on the hot metal.

"I can't believe the headlights are still working," Cooper said.

Britney shut the engine off and yanked the keys from the ignition. Then she got out and shot Ralph and Dennis Adkins once each through the head.

As the rest of the crowd ran away screaming, the two bouncers—Mike Elmore and Philip Cole—stood motionless, staring at Britney.

"Have you lost your fucking mind?" Mike Elmore asked her.

Britney shot him in the face and his head exploded. Then she pointed the gun at Philip Cole and tossed him the keys, which he caught. "Get in the car," she told him. "You're driving."

He got in behind the steering wheel, and Britney got in behind him with the gun to the back of his head.

"Cooper?" Philip said when he recognized the young man on the passenger's side. "Did you put her up to this?"

Cooper shook his head. "Nah, dude. I just met the chick. We were having a conversation, and I told her about you guys giving me grief about Robert Morgan for all these years."

"That's enough," Britney told them. "Shut the fuck up and drive."

Philip started the engine. "Where am I taking us?"

"Turn around, head back to the road, and turn right."

Philip did.

"We're going to one of my crash pads," Britney said. "I have crash pads all throughout the city. So just keep straight. I'll tell you when to turn."

Fifteen minutes later, she told him to turn left, then directed him to a small house in the middle of nowhere. "Now shut the engine off and give me the keys," Britney said.

Philip did.

On the passenger's seat, Cooper turned around. "You're not gonna kill me too, are you?"

"No. I'm doing you a favor."

"Then why can't I have my keys?"

"You'll get your keys back. Don't worry. Now get out of the car. Both of you."

They did, and she forced them to the front door at gunpoint, where she gave Cooper a key and told him to open the door. He did, and she followed them inside, keeping her gun pointed at Philip while closing and locking the door behind her.

Moonlight through the windows illuminated the living room as they crossed it.

In the kitchen, Britney opened a door by the refrigerator, revealing wooden stairs that led to a basement. She flipped a light switch and told them, "Head on down there."

They did, and she followed them down the rickety stairs.

At the bottom, she was pleased to see them look at the heavy chains bolted to the cinderblock walls and the dried blood splattered over the floor in disbelief. "Hope you like what you see."

Philip shot her a look. "This is a torture room."

"Yes, but we're not gonna torture you. Cooper's just gonna chain you up until you apologize to him—and mean it. If we believe your apology is sincere, we'll let you go." Then she told Cooper, "Chain him up."

With Britney's gun pointed at him, Philip did not resist as Cooper led him to a wall and shoved his back against it.

Britney told Philip, "Raise your arms."

He did, and Cooper fastened metal clasps around his wrists. They locked into place with metallic snaps. Then he did the same thing to Philip's ankles.

"What exactly am I apologizing for?" Philip asked.

"You're not," Britney said. "I changed my mind." She walked over to a corner of the room, then returned pushing a rolling medical cart. On a tray atop the cart were numerous surgical instruments and a ball-gag.

"Wait!" Philip implored. Then he told Cooper, "Look, dude. I'm sorry. Okay? I'm sorry. You don't have to torture me."

Britney said, "You don't even know what you're apologizing for."

"Yes, I do."

"Then tell us."

Philip looked at Cooper. "For ostracizing you, I guess. After the whole Robert Morgan thing. After you had him sent to prison."

Britney laughed. "He was raping the neighborhood children. He was fucking you and your little friends in your assholes, and you loved it. Then you got mad at Cooper because he didn't like it."

"We were kids!" Philip said. Then he looked at Cooper again. "Listen, dude. I'm sorry, okay? You gotta believe me."

Britney grabbed the ball-gag and handed it to Cooper. "Gag this piece of shit."

"Wait!" Philip said. "I'm sorry! We were just kids! You gotta—"

Cooper shoved the rubber ball-gag into Philip's mouth, then wrapped its leather strap around his head and buckled it tight.

"Take his shoes off," Britney said.

Cooper did.

Britney kicked Philip's shoes across the room. Then she picked a scalpel up and handed it to Cooper. "Now cut his clothes away. Strip him naked."

Cooper did.

Britney picked the clothes up and tossed them out of the way. Then she pointed her gun at Cooper. "Now start cutting him, but don't start with his face."

"Seriously?"

"Yes. I want you to torture him. If you do it, I'll let you live. If you don't, I'll kill you both."

Cooper shrugged. "I can do that." He slashed a red line across Philip's chest with the scalpel, and Philip shrieked. He also tried speaking, but the ball-gag mangled his speech. Blood dripped from his chest onto the floor.

"Nice work," Britney said. "Now split his scrotum open. Castrate the son of a bitch."

"Are you serious right now?"

"Of course, I'm serious. Don't worry. He won't bleed to death."

Cooper shrugged. "If you say so." Using his left hand, he seized the lower skin of Philip's scrotum. Then he cut it open with the scalpel. More blood started dripping, but not a lot. Philip shrieked and writhed in his chains.

"Now castrate him," Britney said.

Cooper shot her a look. "How do I do it?"

Britney cocked her head, still pointing the gun at his face. "You cut his fucking balls out, dumbass. Don't you know what castration means?"

"Yes, but I've never done it before. I mean, is there something special I need to do?"

"There's a cord," Britney said, "that runs to each testicle. It's called the spermatic cord. Just cut the cord and yank his fucking balls out."

Cooper did, and Philip wailed and thrashed as blood cascaded in abundance.

Turning to Britney, Cooper held the testes up in his left, bloody hand. "Do you want these?"

"No. I want you to eat them."

"What?"

"You heard me."

Cooper looked down at the testicles he was holding. "No way."

Still pointing the gun at his face, Britney cocked her head. "You're telling me no?"

"Look, I'm not eating Philip's disgusting testicles."

"Are you familiar with Eurydice? From Greek mythology?"

Cooper shook his head. "Never heard of him."

"*Her*," Britney corrected. "She was the wife of Orpheus. One day, Eurydice fled a rapist, only to step on a viper and be killed by its poisonous bite. And though a penis is shaped like a serpent, semen—in most cases—isn't poisonous. The irony is that she would have been better off getting raped."

Cooper cast aside the testicles. "Why are you telling me this?"

"Because Eurydice," Britney said, "should have just taken what was coming to her."

Then she shot Cooper and Philip once each through the head in rapid succession, killing them instantly.

She left, driving Cooper's car back to her Ferrari, and going home.

Despite the late hour, Atticus and Eleanor greeted her in the front room of the mansion on Holt Mountain.

"Nice night?" Eleanor asked her.

Britney shrugged. "Not bad." Then she handed Atticus a key. "I need two corpses disposed of at my crash pad on Cherokee Road. One of them's still in chains."

He put the key in his pocket. "You got it."

Eleanor asked her husband, "Can I go with you?"

"Of course."

They left.

Britney turned and headed up the stairs.

CH. 18

"Does it ever get any easier?" Peg asked him.

Austin knew she was talking about the loss of her family. His wife and daughter died in the car crash two years ago, but only six months had passed since her husband and children were murdered by the Ku Klux Klan. "Not really," he said. "I wish I could tell you that it does, but it doesn't."

They were lying on her bed in the dark, with the dog Zoey out in the hallway, scratching on the bedroom door to be let in. Austin had been staying at Peg's house for three days, taking showers with her then putting the same clothes back on. They had been drinking and fucking a lot, and he was trying hard not to fall in love.

"My grandparents died when I was young," Peg said. "I don't even remember one of them, and the other three were gone before I was 10. And I was never really affected by any of that. I mean, it just didn't make me sad. I remember feeling guilty about not being sad, but it was my own death, or the death of my parents, that terrified me. Then I became a parent myself and the dread was magnified and eclipsed by a far greater one—the fear of losing my children. But now that they're gone, it's like I'm not afraid of anything. The worst has already happened. I'm just sort of waiting for the end. Does that make sense?"

"Yes," Austin said. "It does."

She kissed his neck. Then she ran a finger down his cheek to the bone of his jaw. "But these past three days have been a nice distraction, so thanks for that."

"You're welcome." He kissed the top of her head. "And likewise."

Peg rolled over, turned her lamp on, and sat up. From the nightstand, she grabbed their bottle of rum and took a drink.

Austin sat up too, and she handed him the bottle. He took a drink and gave the bottle back.

"I hope you were right," Peg said, "about us possibly seeing our families again in the afterlife."

"Me too."

"Do you believe in Heaven and Hell?"

Austin shrugged. "Sometimes."

She nodded. "Same here. Sometimes I think there might be trillions of different Heavens and different Hells."

"Maybe so."

They passed the bottle back and forth a couple of times, then Peg said, "I was reading a book by Robert Lanza one time. He's a scientist. Ever heard of him?"

"Nope."

"I think he's more of a biologist, actually. He has this theory based on the second law of thermodynamics about where a person's energy goes when they die. He thinks we all exist in our own bubbles of spatiotemporal reality and, that when we die, the bubble pops and we go somewhere else."

"Speaking of going somewhere else," Austin said, "I need to go home and change clothes. You wanna go with me?"

Peg took a drink. "To the Winfield mansion?"

"Yep. You can pack some clothes and bring Zoey, if you want to. It's up to you."

"Sounds good. I'll pack her some food and bring her leash, so I can take her outside to do her business."

"Cool," Austin said.

They got dressed and left.

CH. 19

Justin was reading on Britney's sofa when she returned to the suite at midnight. "You're home early," he said. "I wasn't expecting you back until later than this."

She crossed the suite with her duffel bag and sat down on the bed. "I was out killing motherfuckers and smoking crystal meth."

"Killing motherfuckers?"

"Yes. You didn't think I just wrote about killing people, did you?"

Justin did not respond.

Britney unzipped her duffel bag. "Now I gotta shoot some heroin to come down. Wanna shoot some with me?"

"Nah, I'm good on that."

She laughed. "You're no fun." From the duffel bag, she withdrew a spoon, a bottle of water, and a hypodermic syringe. Then she withdrew a balloon and a cigarette lighter.

Justin looked away, wondering if what she said about killing people was true.

The murders in her fiction did seem to ring with authenticity.

He returned his gaze to Britney. She had a length of nylon tied around her arm and held an end of it between her teeth. Then she found a vein and injected herself.

Moments later, she was unconscious.

Justin shook his head. Then he resumed reading Britney's novel.

CH. 20

Makayla, reading in her father's suite, finished *The Shining* by Stephen King and set the book on the coffee table.

Lemarcus, reading a book about astrophysics next to her on the sofa, said, "It says here that cosmic background radiation, which gives us information about the origins of the universe, will be gone in a trillion years."

"What exactly is cosmic background radiation?"

Lemarcus closed the book and sipped his bourbon. "It's basically electromagnetic radiation from the early stages of the universe. The photons that we see now with the help of satellites are lengthening and will eventually stretch beyond the waves of light. So, if astronomers are still looking in a trillion years, they'll have to use other forms of data."

"That's silly," Makayla said. "There won't even be astronomers in a trillion years."

He laughed. "You're probably right. Not around here, anyway. That's for damned sure. This whole galaxy as we know it will be gone long before that."

"Seriously?"

"Yep. Four billion years from now, the Milky Way's gonna collide with our neighbor, Andromeda, and the spiral galaxies as we know them will not survive. They're gonna crash head-on and fly through each other, leaving starry tendrils in their wakes. For eons, they'll continue to come together and fly apart, scrambling stars and constellations until, eventually, after another billion years, they'll merge into a giant elliptical galaxy. We'll be long gone, of course, but any life forms still around will be treated to some awesome cosmic choreography."

Makayla sipped from the bottle of Sprite she was holding. "I hope Mom's still burning in Hell when that happens."

Her father cracked a grin. "I'm sure she will be." Then he looked down at the book she had finished. "So, what did you think of *The Shining*, anyway?"

"Not bad, but I like the movie better."

"Spoken like a true eight-year-old."

She laughed. "Whatever, geezer! You said you like the movie better, too."

Lemarcus sipped his bourbon. "Yeah, I actually do. It's a good book, but I like the movie better. A lot of people say that books are always better, but that's not always true. *Fight Club, Forrest Gump, No Country for Old Men, Jackie Brown, The Exorcist*—those are just a few."

Makayla set her Sprite down and picked up *The Shining*. "I need to take this back to Britney and get something else."

"Whatchu gonna read next?"

"Not sure. She has a lot of books over there. I'll probably grab a Dean Koontz instead of another Stephen King."

"Have you read *Twilight Eyes*?"

"Nope. What's that one about?"

Lemarcus sipped his bourbon. "A psychic teenage boy who can see monsters hiding amongst us. He joins a carnival and then decides to wage war against the monsters."

"That sounds cool." Makayla rose from the sofa. "I'll see if she has it." She left, leaving her father's door unlocked so she could get back in.

In the hallway, she passed her own suite next door, then Justin's suite, and then stopped at Britney's door and knocked on it.

Moments later, Justin opened the door. "Hello, Makayla. Come on in."

She stepped inside—and saw Britney unconscious on the bed with a needle stuck in her arm. "Is she okay?"

"Yeah, she does this all the time. Smokes meth or crack to get high, then shoots heroin to come down. She'll be fine. You here for another book?"

"Yep." Makayla returned *The Shining* to its place on a shelf, then found *Twilight Eyes* soon thereafter.

When she left, Justin followed her out into the hallway and closed the door behind him. "Can I talk to you for a minute?"

"Sure," Makayla said. "What's up?"

Justin looked both ways down the long, empty hallway. "I know you're only eight, but you seem smarter than me, and I'm twice your age. So, I wanna ask you something. Does this place seem...strange to you? Not the place itself, but the people."

"Of course," Makayla said. "They're all insane."

Justin laughed. "I believe you're right."

"I know I'm right. I sneak around this place at night, after my dad falls asleep, and you wouldn't believe some of the things I've seen. Especially down in the basement. We're living with a bunch of lunatics. They do black magic down there, human sacrifices, all kinds of stuff."

"Seriously?"

"Yes. There's a lot more people living here than just the ones we see on a daily basis."

Down the hallway, the elevator doors opened, and Makayla watched Austin and a woman with a small dog on a leash step out into the hallway. As they approached, the dog looked up at Makayla and strained on its pink leash.

"A Yorkie-poo!" Makayla said. "She's beautiful!"

Austin said, "Her name is Zoey. I think she likes you." Then he looked at Justin and asked Makayla, "Who's your friend?"

Before she could respond, Justin introduced himself. "I'm Justin, a friend of your sister. I've heard a lot about you, Austin, and she showed me your picture. It's nice to meet you."

Austin cocked his head. "Is Britney here?"

"Yes," Justin said. "She's asleep."

Austin asked Makayla, "Where's your dad?"

Makayla—kneeling down and petting Zoey while the Yorkie-poo licked her other hand—said, "Dad's asleep, too." Then she rose and looked up at the woman.

"This is Peg," Austin told her. "One of my friends from a support group." Then he told Peg, "This is Makayla, the daughter of my friend Lemarcus I was telling you about."

Peg smiled. "It's nice to meet you, Makayla. I've heard you're awfully smart for an eight-year-old."

"It's nice to meet you, too."

Justin told Peg, "And you heard correctly. I'm 16, and Makayla reads twice as fast as I do."

Peg asked Makayla, "Your dad's an English teacher, right?"

"Yes. Well, he used to be. Now we live here, and he works for Austin's dad."

Down the hallway, the elevator doors opened again, and Makayla watched Atticus and Eleanor step out into the hallway and approach them.

"Welcome home," Eleanor told Austin, smiling. "We saw you on the surveillance screen and wanted to say hello." Then the old woman looked at Peg and said, "Who's your friend?"

"I'm Peg, Austin's friend from a support group."

"Support group?"

"Yes," Peg said. "'Loss of child,' 'loss of spouse,' that sort of thing."

"Oh, dear. I'm sorry to hear that. I'm Eleanor, and this is my husband, Atticus."

"It's nice to meet you," Peg said.

"It's nice to meet you, too." Eleanor bent down to pet the Yorkie-poo, but Zoey backed away. Eleanor rose and asked Peg, "Will you be staying for a while?"

Peg nodded. "For a few days, anyway. Austin was nice enough to invite me to get out of the house for a while."

"Great!" Eleanor said. "I'll cook dinner tomorrow evening, and I'd like all of you to come."

"All of us?" Austin asked.

Eleanor laughed. "Well, not the whole family, of course. But I'll invite your mom and dad. And your sister. If you see her before I do, tell Britney that dinner will be ready at 7 o'clock."

Austin nodded. "Okay."

Justin said, "I'll tell her. I'm sure I'll see Britney before you two."

"Thank you, Justin," Eleanor said. Then she told Makayla, "And don't forget to tell your father. I want you and Lemarcus at the dinner, too."

"Okay. I'll tell him."

Atticus put an arm around Eleanor's shoulders. "We still have a few chores to finish up."

"I know."

As the old couple turned and headed back toward the elevator, Austin led Peg and Zoey to his suite down the hall.

Alone again, Justin told Makayla, "You're right. This place is full of freaks."

CH. 21

To Justin's left, Britney woke up next to him on the bed. He had been reading one of her books, and he closed it.

The needle was still in her arm, and she yanked it out. "What time is it?"

"Almost 4 o'clock in the morning. How are you feeling?"

"Not bad, but I need a fucking drink." She got up, mixed a drink at the minibar, then brought it back to the bed and sat down.

"Eleanor's cooking dinner tomorrow night," Justin said. "She wanted me to tell you."

"Cool." Britney sipped her drink. "Eleanor's a good cook." She set her glass on the nightstand and grabbed her duffel bag.

"I met your brother tonight," Justin said.

Britney shot him a look. "Austin's home?"

"Yep. He had a woman with him named Peg from a support group. She seemed nice."

Britney shook her head. "No woman will ever be nice enough for my brother. Not in my opinion, anyway. But she won't last. They never do." She unzipped her duffel bag.

"Can I ask you a question?"

"Of course."

"Earlier, when you said you kill people, were you serious?"

"Of course I was serious. And you're gonna start killing people with me. That's why I brought you here."

Justin set the book down. "I'm not killing anyone."

Britney laughed, withdrawing another syringe from her duffel bag. "Are you telling me no?"

"I guess. I mean, maybe I should just head on back to Charleston."

"Not happening," Britney said, raising the syringe. Then she slammed the needle into his thigh through his pants and pressed the plunger.

"Jesus fucking Christ, Britney! What the hell was that? Goddamn heroin?"

"No. Rocuronium. It's a fast-acting paralytic."

Moments later, Justin couldn't move.

CH. 22

Makayla's voice: "Wake up, Dad." Lemarcus opened his eyes. His daughter stood before him in the suite's living space. "We're gonna be late."

"Late?"

"Eleanor's cooking us dinner. Don't you remember?"

Lemarcus rubbed his eyes. "Yeah, I remember. Is it 7 o'clock already?"

"Almost. We have like five more minutes."

He rose from the sofa, grabbed his bottle of whiskey, and took a drink. "Ready when you are."

Makayla looked at his bottle. "Are you taking that with you?"

"Yep. If those white folks don't want me drinking at their dinner party, they can kiss my fuckin' ass. Pardon my language."

Makayla laughed. "It's okay, Dad. Your language doesn't offend me."

They took the stairs down to the first floor and made their way to the dining room, where Wesley Winfield sat at the head of a table for ten. His wife Nora sat at the far end, and there were four chairs on either side of the table.

Three of the chairs on the opposite side were occupied. Austin sat in the chair on the corner nearest his father. Next to him sat Peg, Austin's friend from a support group whom Lemarcus had met earlier that day. Britney sat next to Peg, with an empty chair on the corner between Britney and her mother.

The old married couple—Atticus and Eleanor— occupied two of the four chairs on this side. Eleanor sat in the chair on the corner nearest Nora, with Atticus sitting to her right. After Makayla chose the chair next to Atticus, Lemarcus sat down next to Makayla in the chair on the corner nearest Wesley, with Austin seated across from him.

"Glad you could make it," Austin told him. "Let me hit that whiskey."

Lemarcus handed him the bottle. Austin took a drink and gave the bottle back.

"Where's Justin?" Makayla asked Britney.

Lemarcus looked around. Nine of the ten chairs were occupied, but the table had not been set for ten—only nine.

"He couldn't make it," Britney replied. "Justin's not feeling well, but he told me to tell you that he'll be with us in spirit."

Soon thereafter, servants brought plates of mashed potatoes and bowls of stew, and they started eating.

Makayla told Eleanor, "This stew is delicious."

"Thank you! I made it in the Crock Pot. It's an Italian veal stew called spezzatino."

Lemarcus said, "I've never had veal before. It's very tasty. Veal is lamb, right?"

"No, Dad," Makayla said. "Veal comes from young cows. Lamb comes from young sheep."

"Smart girl," Wesley Winfield said.

"Peg," Britney said, "I heard you met my brother in a support group."

"Yep. Sure did."

"What kind of support group?"

"Loss of child. Loss of spouse. That kind of thing."

Britney sipped her drink. "So, which did you lose? A child or a spouse?"

"Both. I lost my husband and two children six months ago."

"Damn. That's brutal. How old were your kids?"

"My son was seven, and my daughter was four. I have some photos on my phone. Would you like to see them?"

"Sure!"

Peg showed Britney some photos on her phone, and Britney pointed at one. "That was your husband?"

"Yes. His name was Malcolm."

Britney shot Lemarcus a look from across the table—and winked.

What the fuck is this bitch winking at me for? Lemarcus thought.

"Beautiful family," Britney told Peg. "I'm sorry for your loss." Then she looked at Lemarcus and winked again, smiling.

Crazy fucking bitch, Lemarcus thought.

By the conclusion of dinner, he had been ready to leave the room for quite some time.

CH. 23

To his left, Peg rose from Austin's sofa in his suite. "It's almost midnight. I should take Zoey outside to pee."

He looked up from his book of crossword puzzles. "Want me to go with you?"

"No, that's okay. We'll be right back." From the coffee table, she grabbed Zoey's leash, which was pink like the dog's collar. "Zoey," she said. "You ready to go potty?"

The Yorkie-poo wagged her tail.

"Sit," Peg said. When Zoey sat, she attached the leash to Zoey's collar, and then someone knocked on the door.

Austin got up, opened the door, and saw his sister standing in the hallway. "Hello, Britney. Come on in."

Britney stepped inside, nodded at Peg, then looked down at her dog, but didn't acknowledge it.

Peg led the Yorkie-poo into the hallway and closed the door.

"What can I do for you?" Austin asked.

Britney asked, "What the fuck are you doing with that skank?"

"Skank?"

"Yes. She's an ugly fucking skank."

"She's not a skank. She's a very attractive woman—with a college education. She was married to a judge, for God's sake."

Britney laughed. "She married a black man, dumbass."

"What the fuck does that have to do with anything?"

"It means you're not her type, Austin. She likes the dark meat. Maybe you should hook her up with Lemarcus."

"Whatever, Britney. Was there something you needed? Otherwise, this conversation is over."

She withdrew a bag of white powder from her pocket and held it up. "Wanna shoot some heroin?"

"No thanks. I quit."

Britney laughed again. "Quit? You're no fun."

She left.

Austin closed the door, but left it unlocked for Peg and for Zoey.

CH. 24

In her father's suite, Makayla finished *Twilight Eyes* and closed it. "You were right, Dad. This book was amazing."

Lemarcus, reading an Ella Fitzgerald biography next to her on the sofa, sipped from his bottle of bourbon. "Cool. Whatchu gonna read next?"

"Not sure." She rose from the sofa. "I'm gonna take this back to Britney and grab something else."

She left, resisting an urge to knock on Justin's door as she passed it, then stopped at Britney's door and knocked.

Moments later, Britney opened the door. "Hello, Makayla. Come on in."

Makayla stepped inside, returned *Twilight Eyes* to its place on a shelf, and then began looking for something else. "I think I'm in the mood for a ghost story."

"Nice," Britney said. "Do you believe in ghosts?"

"Yes, I do."

"Yeah, me too." Britney joined her in front of the shelf. "Some people think ghosts are just wishful thinking, that we imagine ghosts to make us feel better, because we miss people after they die, but it isn't true. Ghosts are very real."

"Speaking of feeling better," Makayla said, "have you talked to Justin?"

Britney laughed. "No. And trust me, I don't think Justin's ghost will try to contact me, but his soul lives in all of us, now."

Makayla looked up. "What are you talking about?"

Britney laughed again. "Remember when I told you that Justin was with us in spirit at the dinner party? I lied. He was with us in the flesh, too."

"What do you mean?"

"Justin was in the stew. That wasn't veal. You ate him. And now we're going to eat you."

Makayla tried to run, but Britney grabbed her and slammed her to the floor.

Then she stuck the hypodermic syringe into Makayla's neck and pressed the plunger.

CH. 25

Lemarcus set down the Ella Fitzgerald biography. Then he took a shot of bourbon and rose from the sofa. Damn, he thought. How long has Makayla been gone? Seems like an awfully long time.

From the coffee table, he grabbed his pistol and shoved it into the waistband of the back of his jeans. Then he left the suite and walked to Britney's door down the hallway. He knocked, but no one answered, and he heard no sounds from within. He tried to open the door, but it was locked. On his way back, he knocked on Justin's door, but no one answered, and it was locked also.

Then he passed his own suite and knocked on Austin's door at the end of the hall.

Moments later, Austin opened the door. "What's up, dude? Come on in."

Lemarcus stepped inside. He saw Peg sitting on Austin's sofa with Zoey on her lap.

"What's wrong, man?" Austin asked. "You outta whiskey?"

"Nah, dude. I'm looking for Makayla. She went to your sister's room for a book, and never came back."

"Did you knock on Britney's door?"

"Yep. No one answered. I'm thinking Makayla might be down in the basement."

"The basement?"

"Yeah. She told me she goes down there sometimes, when I'm asleep, and that she's seen some crazy shit down there."

"Have you ever been down there?" Austin asked.

Lemarcus shook his head. "Nah, man."

"Dude, the basement's huge." Austin grabbed his pistol from the coffee table, and shoved it into the waistband of his jeans. "I'll go with you."

Peg got up, also. "Can I go, too?"

Austin shrugged. "I guess, if you want to."

Peg looked down at the Yorkie-poo. "You stay here, Zoey. We'll be right back."

Leaving Zoey in the suite, they all three stepped out into the hallway and headed toward the elevator.

CH. 26

The drug was wearing off, and Makayla could move again, but it did her no good because she hung by a rope from an iron pipe that ran beneath the basement's ceiling. The thick rope was tied around her wrists; she hung with her arms above her head and her feet about a foot off the floor.

The old man Atticus carried her down here after Britney shoved the needle into her neck, then his wife Eleanor stripped her naked. Wesley Winfield tied her up, and now he, his wife Nora, Atticus, Eleanor, and Britney stood around her in a semicircle. All five held knives that looked like ceremonial daggers. Chanting in a language Makayla had never heard, Wesley Winfield stepped closer and raised his knife.

Makayla had always known she was going to die—eventually. But now? So soon? With no time to get used to the idea? Was that even possible?

Yes, she knew. It was possible. This was not a bad dream from which she would wake up on a sofa with her father by her side. She was going to die, and the most she could hope for was a quick death and to wake up in Heaven.

Do they have books in Heaven?

Makayla hoped so. Maybe Heaven was like the Garden of Eden with a library in which she could read and wait for her father. Satan was currently on Earth, she believed, but she also believed his days were numbered—that soon, he would be cast into Hell to burn with her mother through the rest of eternity.

To her left, over the clamor of Wesley's chanting, she heard the creaking of hinges as a door opened. She turned her head.

Austin, Peg, and her father entered the chamber in which she was being held. They didn't say a word as they approached. Then her father raised his gun and shot Wesley four times in the chest before the next round blew his brains out.

"NO!" Nora screamed as her husband's corpse dropped to the floor.

She rushed Lemarcus with her knife raised, still screaming, and he silenced her with a bullet between the eyes.

Nora's knife fell from her hand when her body hit the floor.

Pointing his pistol at Atticus and Eleanor, Lemarcus kicked the knife toward Austin. "Cut Makayla loose," he told him. "I'll keep an eye on these two."

As Austin approached Makayla, Britney ran to Peg, grabbed her by the hair, and pressed the blade to Peg's neck.

Austin drew a gun from the waistband of his jeans and aimed it at his sister. "You can be cool, Britney, and put that fucking knife down, or you can be dead fucking cold."

"Fuck you, Austin! And fuck this skank bitch, too." Britney then sliced Peg's throat wide open and let her drop.

Austin shot his sister between the eyes.

"Traitor!" Eleanor screamed, looking at Austin. "You would choose these filthy strangers over your own family?"

Makayla watched her father shoot Atticus and Eleanor each through the head in rapid succession.

Then he grabbed a knife and cut her loose. By the time she gathered her clothes and put them on, Peg lay dead on the floor in the blood that had gushed from her neck.

"What now?" Lemarcus asked Austin.

"We're leaving. We'll head west. I have some contacts in California."

"I don't have a lot of cash left," Lemarcus said.

"I have plenty of money. We'll be fine. Just don't forget to bring your fake IDs."

"Peg's dog," Makayla said. "The Yorkie-poo. Can she go with us?"

"That's up to your dad," Austin told her.

Makayla looked up at her father. "Can Zoey go with us?"

Lemarcus shrugged. "I guess. But the dog's gonna be your responsibility."

They went upstairs, packed a few things, and left.

Austin drove. Lemarcus rode next to him on the passenger's side.

Makayla rode behind them with the Yorkie-poo by her side. Soon, the dog fell asleep.

We're safe, Makayla thought, stroking Zoey's fur. And you and I are alive at the same time. Everything's fine.

She turned her head and watched the night beyond the glass until her eyes got tired, and then she closed them.

Thanks for reading! Find more transgressive fiction (poems, novels, anthologies) at: Outcast-Press.com Twitter & Instagram: @OutcastPress, @OutcastPress1

Facebook.com/OutcastPress1

~ ~ ~

Email proof of your review to OutcastPress@gmail.com & we'll mail you a free bookmark & stickers!

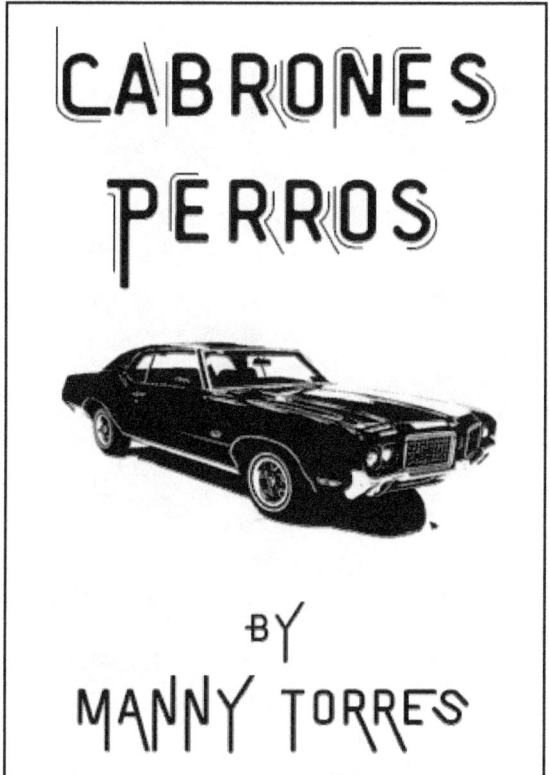

Cabrones Perros is a rum-soaked crime-comedy. From Atlanta, Georgia, to Odyssey, Florida, hitmen (and -women) converge where drugs are cheap and human-trafficking is prevalent. Nolin is the ex-con who can't catch a break besides breaking necks. Shank is set on vengeance against those who killed her family. Upcoming gangstress Shady slides into a turf war with an Eastern-European crime family. This war on the waterside can only end with scorched sand and severed heads.

MORE FROM OUTCAST PRESS

From the greasy spoon to gourmet sit-in, these 20 stories curated by Craig Clevenger (author of *The Contortionist's Handbook, Mother Howl,* and *In Filth It Shall Be Found*) show diners are where heists are plotted, bodies get dumped, and police are tipped off. They host every crime from drug deals to premeditated murder and mob mutiny. It's all fluorescent-lit, fly-riddled entertainment to the drunk, recovering, or wish-they-were.

ABOUT THE AUTHOR

Twitter: @BBowyerAuthor   Facebook: /BrianBowyer99

Brian Bowyer lives and writes in Ohio as a Splatterpunk Award-nominated and Godless Award-winning author. Having lived all through the U.S. while working as a janitor, a banker, a bartender, a bouncer, or a bomb maker for a coal-testing lab, Bowyer has always enjoyed creating transgressive stories and rock music.

Some of Bowyer's influences include Clive Barker, Robert McCammon, Poppy Z. Brite, Richard Laymon, Jack Ketchum, Carson McCullers, and Chuck Palahniuk. His next novel will be set in Los Angeles. You can contact him at Brian.Bowyer@hotmail.com

www.ingramcontent.com/pod-product-compliance
Lightning Source LLC
Chambersburg PA
CBHW022037170626
46808CB00003B/1248